ACCLAIM FOR THE WORKS OF MICHAEL CRICHTON!

"Michael's talent outscaled even his own dinosaurs of *Jurassic Park*. He was the greatest at blending science with big theatrical concepts. . .There is no one in the wings that will ever take his place."
—Steven Spielberg

"Crichton keeps us guessing at every turn."
—*Los Angeles Times*

"[Crichton] marries compelling subject matter with edge-of-your-seat storytelling."
—*USA Today*

"Crackling. . .mysterious . . ."
—*Entertainment Weekly*

"One of the great storytellers of our age. . . What an amazing imagination."
—*New York Newsday*

"Crichton writes vividly."
—*Washington Post*

"Compulsively readable."
—*National Review*

DRUG OF CHOICE

MICHAEL CRICHTON WRITING AS JOHN LANGE™

Odds On
Scratch One
Easy Go
The Venom Business
Zero Cool
Drug of Choice
Grave Descend
Binary

#1 *NEW YORK TIMES* BESTSELLING AUTHOR

MICHAEL CRICHTON

WRITING AS JOHN LANGE™

DRUG OF CHOICE

BLACK STONE
PUBLISHING

Copyright © 1970 by Constant c Productions, Inc. (successor to Centesis Corporation)
Copyright © renewed 2005 by Constant c Productions, Inc.
Copyright © assigned 2013 by Constant c Productions, Inc.
to the John Michael Crichton Trust
Copyright © assigned 2013 by the John Michael Crichton Trust
to CrichtonSun, LLC
All rights reserved under International and Pan-American Copyright Conventions.

CrichtonSun™, *John Lange*™, and *Drug of Choice*™ are trademarks of CrichtonSun, LLC and are used with permission.

No part of this book may be reproduced or used in any manner whatsoever without the express written permission of the copyright owner except for the use of brief quotations in a book review.

This is a work of fiction. Names, characters, places, incidents, notes and bibliographic citations are products of the author's imagination or are used fictitiously and are not to be construed as real. Any resemblance to actual events, locates, organizations or persons, living or dead, is entirely coincidental.

Printed in the United States of America

ISBN 979-8-200-98741-2
Library of Congress Control Number: 2022950454
Fiction / Mystery & Detective / General

Version 1

Blackstone Publishing
31 Mistletoe Rd.
Ashland, OR 97520
www.BlackstonePublishing.com

www.MichaelCrichton.com

FOREWORD
by Sherri Crichton

It is such an honor and pleasure to see the John Lange books freshly and newly published by Blackstone, to reintroduce these books to fans and also present them to a whole new generation of readers.

My husband, Michael Crichton, put himself through Harvard Medical School in the sixties by writing pulp fiction novels. He wrote them as John Lange and Jeffery Hudson before he was published under his own name with *The Andromeda Strain*.

The John Lange books are adventure stories, and you can start to see in them the genius that would, only a few years later, become so apparent. While later in his career Michael made a point of separating his identity from these novels, I suspect he had a lot more affection for them than he showed.

The books are set in the late sixties and seventies and were his tribute to Ian Fleming's James Bond novels and to one of his favorite Alfred Hitchcock films, *To Catch a Thief*; the books are about secret treasures, heists, archaeology, unlikely heroes, seductive and at times treacherous lovers, classic villains, and much more.

I look at these John Lange novels with great affection as I picture Michael studying medicine day and night and writing these fun books over school breaks and holidays. Becoming an author was his dream—not being a doctor—and the John Lange novels truly are a testament to his exotic imagination, places he dreamed of visiting, and above all, they show the birth of Michael as an author.

In an interview from December 2000, Michael shared details of the beginning of his career in the sixties. His comments reveal how he went from John Lange to Michael Crichton:

I was one of those kids who seemed to know very early what I wanted to do. I was driven to writing. I did a lot of it starting around the third grade, when I wrote this enormously long puppet show that had to be typed up by my father with carbon copies so that all the kids could have their parts.

At that time most of the third graders were writing a page, and I had written this very long thing. But I just wanted to do it. I don't know how to explain it any differently.

When I was thirteen or fourteen, I had visited a place in Arizona called Sunset Crater Volcano National Monument; I thought it was extremely interesting and relatively unknown. I complained that people didn't have more knowledge about this place, and my mother and father told me, "Well, why don't you write an article?" I said, "I can't do that." And they said, "No, no, the *New York Times* accepts articles in their Travel section from all kinds of people." So I wrote an article and they published it.

I'd read that only two hundred people in the United States were able to support themselves full time writing books. I thought to be one of two hundred people in the entire country seemed a very difficult group to join. And six thousand doctors graduated every year. That seemed much more doable. But while I was in medical school, I began to write to pay the term bills. I wrote under a pseudonym because the grades you got in those days were very dependent on the evaluation of your teachers, and I was quite convinced that if they knew I was running off to write books, they would think less of me.

The names I chose were John Lange and Jeffery Hudson. John Lange, I drew from my own first name, which is John, and I thought of these books as James Bond thrillers, fairy tales for adults. I associated the books to Andrew Lang, who was an author of Victorian fairy tales, and Jeffery Hudson, who was a little person from the court of Charles I of England and a great adventurer. I thought it would be very entertaining for me to have the name of a little person since I am six nine.

The book I wrote under the name Jeffery Hudson, *A Case of Need*, was optioned for a movie and eventually made by Blake Edwards. It made my life very strange because I was sometimes going to California to talk to the screenwriter, then I'd come back and put on my whites to be in the hospital. There's a bizarre difference between being an impoverished student and then having these periods where I got into limousines and drove around Hollywood. It made me a little crazy. Yet, even when *A Case of Need* won the Edgar Award for Best Mystery and I had to go down to New York to accept the award, no one in the medical school ever found out, which was odd. It showed me how self-centered the institution of medicine really was.

Eventually, I was going to write a nonfiction book, which ultimately was published as *Five Patients*, and I had to go to the dean to get permission to skip certain classes to do this book. He said, "Well, writing a book is very difficult. Do you realize how difficult it is? Have you ever done anything like that?" And at that point I finally thought it was okay, and I said, "Yes, actually, I've written several books."

My next novel to be published was *The Andromeda Strain*; I wrote it in secret, and when [director] Robert Wise bought it to make it as a film, it got publicized that there was this kid in medical school who had sold a book to the movies for a lot of money.

My picture was on the wire services. The story was officially out. Everybody knew. But looking back on it, it was a very free time.

DRUG OF CHOICE

> "The beginning of modern science is also the beginning of calamity."
> KARL JASPERS

> "Give me librium or give me meth!"
> ANON.

TABLE OF CONTENTS

Part I: Coma 1
   1. Angel In Coma 5
   2. By Love Depressed. 18
   3. Tailspin II 32
   4. The Love Next 40
   5. Shine On. 44
   6. Interlude: Sybocyl 50
   7. Advance, INC. 55
   8. The Place To Go. 69
   9. The Best. 74
Part II: Eden. 81
   10. A Feeling Of Power 85
   11. Olive Or Twist? 89
   12. Trippytime. 93
   13. East Of San Cristobal. 101
   14. Gainful Employment. 108
   15. Reversal 121
   16. The Short Sad Lie Of Roger Clark 131
Part III: Madness 139
   17. The Scientific Coming 143
   18. Glow Girl. 155
   19. K Puppy. 163
   20. Eighteenth Nervous Breakdown. 170
   21. It's You, Roger 178
   22. Back In The U.S.S.R. 186
   23. Fools Walk Out 194

PART I
COMA

PART I
COMA

"Shall I tell you what knowledge is? It is to know both what one knows and what one does not know."
SAYING OF CONFUCIUS

1
ANGEL IN COMA

The cop, positioned at the intersection of the Santa Ana Freeway and US 85, saw it all. At three in the afternoon an Angel went past him, hunched over his bike, doing a hundred and ten. The cop later remembered that the Angel had a maniacal grin on his face as he raced forward, weaving among the passenger cars.

The policeman gave chase, light flashing and siren wailing, but traffic was heavy and the Angel managed to keep his distance. He left the freeway in the foothills, and headed north into the mountains, still going more than a hundred miles an hour. The cop followed, but the bike was taking chances, and managed to pull further ahead.

After twenty minutes, the police car came around a bend and the cop saw the bike at the side of the road, lying on its side. The motor was still on, spinning the rear wheel.

The Angel lay sprawled on the ground a short distance away. He had apparently been moving slowly at the time of the accident, because he was unmarked—no cuts, no bruises, no scrapes. He was, however, comatose, and could not be roused.

The policeman checked the pulse, which was strong and regular. He tried for several minutes to awaken the Angel, and then returned to his car to call an ambulance.

Roger Clark, resident in internal medicine, went on duty at the Los Angeles Memorial Hospital at six. When he arrived on the floor, he went to see Baker, the day resident. Baker was in the dressing room, changing from his whites to street clothes. He looked tired.

"How're things?" Clark said, stripping off his sport coat and putting on a white jacket.

"Okay. Not much excitement, except for Mrs. Leaver. She still pulls out her intravenous lines when she thinks nobody's looking."

Clark nodded, stepping to the mirror and straightening his tie.

"And then Henry," Baker said. "He had the DTs this morning, and sat in the corner arguing with the little green men."

"How is he now?"

"We gave him some Librium, but watch him. One of the nurses said he felt her up last night."

"Who's that?"

"Alice."

"Alice? He must really be hallucinating if he felt *her* up."

"Well, just don't mention it to Alice. She's very sensitive."

Baker finished dressing, lit a cigarette, and rapidly went through the status of the other patients. Nothing much had changed since Clark had gone off duty twenty-four hours before.

"Oh," Baker said. "Almost forgot a new admission. One of those Hell's Angels. The cops brought him in after he had a motorcycle accident. He was comatose and he hasn't come out yet."

"You ask for a neurological consult?"

"Yeah, but they probably won't get around to it until morning."

"What's his status now?"

"We did the usual stuff. Skull films negative, CSF normal, chest films okay, EEG vaguely abnormal, but nothing specific. All his reflexes are there."

"Cardiorespiratory depression?"

"Nope. He's just fine. To look at him, you'd think he was asleep."

"You treating?"

"No, we're waiting for the consult. Let the neuro boys play around with him for a while."

"Okay. Anything else?"

"No. That's it." Baker smiled. "See you tomorrow."

When he was alone, Clark made a quick round of the wards, checking on the patients. Everyone seemed in pretty good shape. When he came to the comatose Angel, he paused.

The patient was young, in his early twenties. Nobody had washed him since admission; his hair was greasy, his face was unshaven and streaked with grit, and his fingernails were rimmed with black. He lay quietly in bed, not moving, breathing slowly and easily. Clark checked him over, listening to the heart, tapping out the reflexes. He could find nothing wrong. They had put an intravenous line into him, and had catheterized him in case of urinary retention. The catheter tube led to a bottle on the floor. He looked at it.

The urine was bright blue.

Frowning, he held the bottle up to the light and looked closely. It was an odd, vivid blue, almost fluorescent.

What turned urine blue?

He went back to the desk, hoping to catch Baker and ask

about the urine, but Baker was gone. Sandra, the night nurse, was there.

"Were you on duty when they brought that Angel in?"

"Arthur Lewis? Yes."

"What happened?"

Sandra shrugged. "The police brought him into the emergency ward. They figured he'd had an accident, so they took him up to X-ray and checked him over. No broken bones, nothing. All the enzymes and electrolytes came back normal. The EW couldn't figure it out, so they shipped him up here. It's all very mysterious. He was going a hundred before the accident, but the police think he slowed way down before it happened. The policeman who found him said it was just as if he had suddenly fallen asleep."

"Ummm," Clark said. He bit his lip. "What about his urine?"

"What about it?"

"Has it always been blue?"

Sandra frowned and left the desk. She went into the ward and looked at the bottle, then returned. "I've never seen anything like that," she said.

"Neither have I."

"What turns urine blue?"

"I was just wondering the same thing," Clark said. "Why don't you call down to neurology and say the guy is still in a coma, but urinating blue. Maybe that'll bring them up."

Ten minutes later, Harley Spence, Chief of Neurology, appeared on the seventh floor, panting slightly. He was a white-haired man in his middle fifties, very proper in a three-piece suit.

His first words to Clark were: "Urinating blue?"

"That's right, sir."

"How long has this been going on?"

"Apparently it just started, within the last few minutes."

"Fascinating," Spence said. "Perhaps a new kind of porphyria. Or some idiosyncratic drug reaction. Whatever it is, it's definitely reportable."

Clark nodded. In his mind, he saw the journal article: "H.A. Spence: Unusual Urinary Pigment in a Comatose Man. Report of a Case."

They walked to the patient's bed. Clark ran through the story while Spence began his examination. Arthur Lewis, twenty-four, unemployed, first admission through the EW in a coma after a motorcycle accident . . .

"Motorcycle accident?" Spence said.

"Apparently."

"He's unmarked. Not a scratch on him. Would you say that's likely?"

"No, sir, but that's the police story."

"Ummm."

Muttering to himself, Spence conducted his neurological examination. He worked briskly at first, and then more slowly. Finally he scratched his head.

"Remarkable," he said. "Quite remarkable. And this urine—bright blue."

Spence stared at the bottle, hesitated, then turned to Clark. "What makes urine blue?"

Clark shrugged.

Spence shook his head, put the bottle down. He stepped back from the patient and looked at him.

"Jesus Christ, blue piss," he said. "What a patient."

And he walked off.

The metabolic boys came around an hour later; they collected several samples for analysis, amid a lot of vague talk about tubular secretory rates and refractile indices; Clark listened to them until he was sure they had no idea what was going on. Then, as he was leaving, one of them said, "Listen, Rog, what do you make of this?"

"I don't make anything of it," Clark said.

"Do you think it's a drug thing? You're the local expert."

Clark smiled. "Hardly." He had done two years of drug testing at Bethesda, but it had been boring work, measuring excretion and metabolism of experimental drugs in animals and, occasionally, in human subjects. He had only done it because it got him out of the army.

"Well, could it be a bizarre drug reaction?"

Clark shrugged. "It could. Of course it could. Even a common drug like aspirin can produce strange reactions in certain people."

Someone else said, "What about an entirely new drug?"

"Like what?"

"I don't know. But these Angels will take anything in a capsule. Remember the guy we got who had swallowed a hundred birth control pills?"

"I don't think that birth control pills would turn—"

"No, no, of course not. But what if this is some entirely new drug, some new thing like STP or THC or ASD?"

"Possible," Clark said. "Anything's possible." On that note, the metabolic boys went back to the labs, clutching their urine samples, and Clark went back to work.

Word of the Angel quickly spread through the hospital. A constant stream of doctors, residents, interns, students, nurses, and orderlies appeared on the floor to look at Arthur Lewis and his urine bottle. During all this time, the patient continued to sleep peacefully. Repeated attempts to rouse him by calling his name, shaking him, or pinching him were unsuccessful.

At midnight, everything on the floor seemed quiet, and Clark went to bed. He stretched out on the cot in the resident's room, fully dressed, and fell asleep almost immediately.

At five in the morning, he got a call from Sandra. She needed him on the seventh floor; she couldn't say more. She sounded frightened, so he went right up.

When he arrived, he found Sandra talking to an immense, bearded man in black leather. Though all the lights on the floor had been turned off except the nightlights, the man wore sunglasses. He had a huge naked angel painted on the back of his leather jacket, and on his hand was a tattoo of a heart pierced by an arrow. Underneath, in gold lettering, it said "Twat."

Clark walked up to him. "I'm Dr. Clark. Can I help you?"

Sandra gave a sigh of relief and sat down. The Angel turned to Clark, looked him up and down. He was a head taller than Clark.

"Yeah, man. You can help me."

"How?"

"You can let me see Artie-baby."

"I'm afraid that's not possible."

"Come on, not possible. What is this not possible shit? You sound like a doctor."

"I am a doctor."

"Then you can let me see Artie-baby. All the time, this one keeps saying she can't let me see him because she's not a doctor. So okay, I buy it, right? It's a slide, but I buy it. Now you start in. What is this?"

"Look," Clark said, "it's five in the morning. Visiting hours don't begin until—"

"Visiting hours are for creeps, man."

"I'm sorry. We have certain rules here."

"Yeah, but you know what happens if I come visiting hours? I see all the sickies, and it makes me depressed, you know? It's a down, a real bummer. But now it's dark."

"That's true."

"Yeah, so okay. Right?"

"I'm sorry. Your friend is in a coma now. You can't see him."

"Little Jesus? In a coma? Naw: he wouldn't do a thing like that."

Clark said, "Little Jesus?"

"That's his name, man. He had the crucifixion thing, you know. Every trip, he wants to get nailed. His bag: too much money, he had an unhappy childhood."

Not knowing what else to say, Clark said, "You'd better go now. Come back in the morning."

"I'll be flying by then, man. Soon as I leave, I'm flying."

Clark paused. "Does your friend also fly?"

"Sure, man. All the time. He doesn't like his momma, see, so he does a lot of flying. He saw a shrink, too, but that wasn't as good as a long flight."

"What was he flying?"

"You name it Dope, Gold, Mishra, glue, acid when he was up to it, B's all the time, goofies . . ."

"Did he ever try anything really unusual?"

The Angel frowned. "You got a line on something?"

"No," Clark said. "Just wondered."

"Naw, he was pretty straight. Never shot stuff, even. He's the oral type, you know." The Angel paused. "Now how about it. Do I see him, or what?"

Clark shook his head. "He's in a coma."

"You keep talking this coma crap."

There was a moment of silence, and the Angel reached into his pocket. Clark heard a metallic *click* as the switchblade snapped open. The knife glinted in the light.

"I don't want to call the police," Clark said.

"I don't want to carve your guts out. Now lead the way. I just wanna see him, and then I'll leave. Right?"

Clark felt the tip against his stomach. He nodded.

They went into the ward. The Angel stood at the foot of the bed and watched Arthur Lewis for several minutes. Then he reached into his pocket, fumbled, and frowned. He whispered, "Shit. I forgot it."

"Forgot what?"

"Nothing. Shit."

They went back outside.

"Were you bringing him something?" Clark asked.

"No, man. Forget it, huh?"

The Angel stepped to the elevator. Clark watched him as he got in.

"One last thing," the Angel said. "Cool it with the security guards, or we'll have blood in the lobby."

Clark said cheerfully, "You can see him tomorrow, if you like. Visiting hours from two to three-thirty."

"Man, he won't be here that long."

"His coma is quite deep."

"Man, don't you understand? He isn't in no coma."

The doors closed, and the elevator descended.

"I'll be damned," Clark said, to no one in particular. He went back to bed.

Visit rounds began at ten. The visit today was Dr. Jackson, a senior staff member of the hospital. Clark disliked Jackson, and always had. The feeling was mutual.

Jackson was a tall man with short black hair and a sardonic manner. He made little cracks as he accompanied Clark and the interns around from patient to patient. Late in the morning, they came to Arthur Lewis. Clark presented the case, summarizing the now-familiar story of the motorcycle accident, and the police, the admission through the emergency ward . . .

Jackson interrupted him before he finished. "That man isn't comatose. He's asleep."

"I don't think so, sir."

"You mean to tell me," Jackson said, "that that son-of-a-bitch lying there is in a coma?"

"Yes, sir. The chief of neurology, Dr. Spence, thought so too. He saw the patient—"

"Spence is an old fart. Step aside." He pushed past the interns and stepped to the head of the bed. He peered closely at Lewis, then turned to Clark.

"Watch closely, doctor. This is how you wake a sleeping I patient."

Clark suppressed a smile, and managed a solemn nod.

Jackson bent over Arthur Lewis.

"Mr. Lewis, Mr. Lewis."

The patient did not stir.

"Wake up, Mr. Lewis."

No reaction.

Jackson shook the patient's head gently, then with increasing force. There was no response.

"Mr. Lew-is. Time to get up . . ."

He continued this for several moments, and then, suddenly, slapped Arthur Lewis soundly across the face.

Clark stepped forward. "Sir, I don't think—"

At that moment, Arthur Lewis blinked his eyes, opened them, and smiled.

Jackson stepped back from the bed with a grin of triumph. "Exactly, Dr. Clark. You don't think. This man is simply a heavy sleeper, difficult to rouse. My youngest son is the same way."

He turned to the patient. "How do you feel?"

"Great," Arthur Lewis said.

"Have a good sleep?"

"Yeah, great." He sat up. "Where am I?"

"You're in the LA Memorial Hospital, where the resident staff believes that there is something wrong with you."

"Me? Wrong with me? I feel great."

"I'm sure you do," Jackson said, with a quick glance at Clark. "Would you mind walking around for us?"

"Sure, man." The Angel started to get up, then stopped. He felt under the sheets. "Hey, what's going on here? Somebody's been fooling with my—"

At that moment, for the first time, Clark remembered the blue urine. He moved around to the side of the bed and picked up the bottle. "By the way, Dr. Jackson," he said, "there is one unsolved question here. This man's urine. It's blue."

Clark held up the bottle.

"It is?" Jackson said, frowning.

Clark looked at the bottle. The urine was yellow.

"Well," he said lamely, "it was."

"Isn't that interesting," Jackson said, with a pitying smile.

"Hey, listen," the Angel said. "Get this damned tube outa me. It feels funny. What kinda pervert did a thing like that, anyhow?"

Jackson rested a reassuring hand on the patient's shoulder. "We'll take care of it right away. Just lie back for a minute.

As long as you're here, you might as well have lunch with the other patients."

The rounds group moved off to the next case. The interns were muttering among themselves. Clark stared at the floor.

"I swear to you, sir. Last night his urine was bright blue. I saw it; Dr. Spence saw it; the metabolic boys saw—"

"At this moment," said Dr. Jackson, "I am perfectly willing to believe that you saw polka-dot urine. In this hospital, *anything* is possible."

The patient, Arthur Lewis, was discharged at 1:00 p.m. Before he left, Clark talked with him. The patient remembered nothing about a motorcycle accident, or the police. He claimed he had been sitting in his room, smoking a cigarette, when he fell asleep. He awoke in the hospital; he remembered nothing in between. When Clark asked if he had ever urinated blue before, the Angel gave him a funny look, laughed, and walked away.

There were jokes about Clark at lunch that day, and for several weeks afterward. But eventually it blew over, and was forgotten. For Clark, there was only one really disturbing aspect to the whole situation.

The day Arthur Lewis was discharged, Clark had stopped at the front desk on his way home, and talked to the lobby staff.

"I hope there wasn't any trouble about that Angel in here last night," he said.

"Oh, he was discharged this morning," a receptionist said.

"No, I mean his friend. A huge guy. Came up to the seventh floor at five a.m. with a switchblade."

"Friend?"

"Yes. Another Angel."

"At five in the morning?" the receptionist said.

"Yes."

"I was on duty all night. There was no Angel. I do remember an awfully big man—"

"That's him. Very big man."

"—but he was wearing a sport coat and turtleneck. And he had a little briefcase. Very pleasant-looking man."

Clark frowned. "You're sure?"

The receptionist smiled in a friendly way. "Quite sure, Dr. Clark."

"Well, that's very peculiar."

"Yes," she said, with a slow nod. "It is."

2
BY LOVE DEPRESSED

Her name was Sharon Wilder, and she was quick to point out it was her real name: "Everything about me," she would say, licking her lips, "is real." Certainly there were enough bikini photographs of her on magazine covers around the world to verify her claim. And her agent, an ex-Marine named Tony Lafora, was often heard to say, "Sharon is a very real person. A very real person."

She had made just one film, a sexy robbery story set on the Riviera called *Fast Buck*. Her role had made her famous overnight. Sharon Wilder was twenty-one, five feet six, black-haired, black-eyed, full-lipped, lush—and real.

One cynical reporter wrote of her "rising young talents," but mostly, the press was cordial, and the studios, directors, and photographers were nothing short of ecstatic. In the months after her film opened, press coverage of Sharon Wilder was staggering. She appeared twice on the cover of *Life*, once on *Look*, once on *Newsweek*, three times on *Cosmopolitan*. An article about her and the Hollywood image-making process appeared in *Harper's*. She modeled Pucci for *Vogue*.

The week she appeared on the cover of *Time*, she was wheeled into the emergency ward of the LA Memorial Hospital. It was nine in the evening, and she was in a coma. The medical resident on duty was Roger Clark.

Clark could not have been more astonished. At the time, he was sipping coffee and discussing a new case of chicken pox with an intern. A nurse had come up to him and said, "Dr. Clark, you'd better hurry."

"What is it?"

"The reporters."

"What reporters?"

"They're all out in the lobby. They want to know about Sharon Wilder."

"Sharon Wilder? I don't know anything about her."

A moment later, sirens howling, the ambulance pulled up by the EW and the orderlies wheeled her in. Clark took one look and told the intern to get started on her, to keep the airway clear and check for shock; it was probably an overdose of something. He remained with her long enough to see there was no immediate danger, and then went out to see the reporters. There were a dozen or so, all talking furiously, grabbing every doctor in sight. Clark clapped his hands for their attention. Several flashbulbs popped. He announced that Sharon Wilder had just arrived, and was being examined. They would be told developments as they occurred; in the meantime, would they please wait outside?

They did not budge.

"Come on, Doc. What's the story? Overdose?"

"Barbiturates? Was it barbiturates?"

"LSD?"

"Is it true she slit her wrists?"

"How does she look? You seen her? She pale, or what?"

"OD? Barbs?"

Clark shook his head, said he had not completed his examination, and repeated that they would be told immediate developments. The questions continued. Finally he promised a preliminary report within fifteen minutes. That seemed to quiet them. Grudgingly, they filed outside.

He went back to the EW.

There were three nurses undressing Sharon Wilder and putting a gown on her. The intern was standing by the wall, watching and sweating slightly.

"God, she's beautiful," he said.

Clark frowned. It was true: she looked peaceful and gentle, as if asleep. It was not the way a usual overdose patient looked. Someone with a bottle of phenobarbital sloshing in his stomach was sick: he was pale, gray, ill-looking with a thready pulse and labored respirations.

He knew, even before he checked her pulse and blood pressure, that it would be normal. The entire examination, in fact, was normal.

He began to have an odd feeling.

When he saw that one of the sheets had been stained blue, he stopped the examination.

"Harry," he said to the intern. "Call Dr. Jackson."

"What do you want that bastard for?"

"Call him."

Harry looked puzzled, and left. He returned some minutes later, with Jackson at his side.

"I thought you would be interested," Clark said to Jackson. "Does she look asleep?"

"Yes, but she's not."

"Why do you say that?"

"These film people. It's sure to be an overdose of something."

Clark shrugged. "Pulse is 74 and strong. Respirations are

18 and regular. Blood pressure is good, no localizing signs, no distress."

"That doesn't mean anything," Jackson said irritably. "You should know that. She may be in the early stages of narcosis, and it may progress in the next few hours."

Clark showed him the blue spot on the sheets.

"Idiopathic drug reaction," Jackson said, not blinking. "If I were you, doctor, I'd stop making such a mystery of this and treat the patient. Pump her stomach and get on with it."

And he walked out.

When he was alone, Clark shook the girl's head back and forth, and said, "Sharon, Sharon . . ." in her ear.

She did not respond.

He continued this for several minutes, then, looking around hesitantly, he slapped her hard across her beautiful high cheekbones.

He waited.

Nothing happened.

"Gentlemen, I can report at this time that Miss Wilder is being examined and treated. She is comatose for reasons which are not clear at this time, but her condition at present is stable."

"What's the story? Was it an overdose?"

"We have no information on that."

"Did she hit her head? Did she have a fight?"

"There are no signs of trauma."

"Of what?"

"Injury. No signs of physical injury."

"Is it true she was drunk when she came in?"

"We have no reason to believe so."

"Was it LSD?"

"Almost certainly not."

"How long will she be in the hospital?"

"It's impossible to predict."

"Is she on the critical list?"

"Not at this time."

A nurse came up and whispered in his ear that there was a woman in the emergency ward who claimed to be Miss Wilder's secretary.

Clark nodded, said to the reporters, "That's all for now," and walked back with the nurse to the EW.

Gertrude Finch looked like a giant toad. She was an enormous woman, squat, heavyset, wearing a green print dress. She appeared to be about fifty years old, and very frightened.

"I understand you're Miss Wilder's secretary."

"That's right, Doctor. Her special assistant, you might say."

"I see. You found her?"

"That's right, Doctor. She was lying on her bed, on her back, you know, all dressed up for her date. But out like a light. Her date was downstairs, so I shook her to wake her up. She didn't wake. So I called the ambulance."

"Were there any pills around? Any bottles of medication?"

"No, nothing. A glass of water by the bed, but no bottles."

"Had she taken any medicines recently?"

"Well, she had this sunburn ointment, that she flew in special from Paris."

"But no drugs?"

"No, Doctor."

"Had she been depressed? Unhappy? Moody?"

"No, nothing like that. She was always in good spirits, you might say. She was getting ready to start another picture next month."

Clark took out his notebook. "Do you know who her doctors are?"

Gertrude Finch nodded. "There's her regular doctor. He's Dr. Callaway, in Beverly Hills. But she hasn't seen him for almost a year. And then her psychiatrist, Dr. Shine. He's a hypnotist actually, but he has some kind of degree, I don't know. And then her dermatologist, Dr. Vorhees. He's the one who prescribed the sunburn cream."

Clark wrote it down. "Anyone else?"

"Well, no, except for her dates."

"She's been dating doctors?"

"Just one. He doesn't practice; he's in research."

Clark needed to know anyone who might have given her drugs. "What's his name?"

"Let me think." Miss Finch stared at the floor, frowning. "It's a real funny name. You have a cigarette?"

Clark didn't, but the nurse did. Miss Finch lit it and puffed as she stared at the floor. Finally, she snapped her fingers.

"George Washington. That's it."

"What's so funny about that name?"

"His middle initial," said Miss Finch, "is K. George K. Washington. I'd call that a very peculiar name."

Clark wrote it down, tore the page out of his notebook, and gave it to Harry, the intern.

"Get hold of these people. Find out if any of them have prescribed medicines for Miss Wilder."

Harry left.

"I do hope she's all right," Miss Finch said. "We're all quite attached to her. I was talking to Godfrey, the cook, about her and we both said we were very attached to her." She bit her lip.

"What's the matter?"

"Well, it's Godfrey. What he said."

"What did he say?"

"Well, when they carried her downstairs and out to the ambulance, he saw her and said, 'Mark my words, she has sleeping sickness. African sleeping sickness.'"

"That's very unlikely," Clark said.

"Oh, thank God, I was so worried," Miss Finch said, and burst into tears.

Clark went back to check on Sharon Wilder, but her condition was unchanged. Gastric lavage and emptying of stomach contents had disclosed no material of any sort, not even particles of food.

Clark reported to the press that the patient's status was unchanged; the reporters took this lack of news with ill grace. Talking with them, he had the distinct impression they didn't care whether she got better or worse, just so she changed.

Returning to the EW, he had an idea. He went over to Gertrude Finch.

"Miss Finch, where is Sharon Wilder's purse?"

"Her purse?"

"Yes."

"I have it here. Why?"

"With your permission, I'd like to examine it. We might get some clue as to what she took to put her in a coma."

Miss Finch hesitated. "I don't know . . ."

"This could be important."

"Well, all right."

Together, they went into a conference room and emptied the contents. There was a suede wallet with a hundred dollars, a driver's license, two gasoline credit cards, and three pictures of herself. There were two kinds of eye shadow, five kinds of lipstick, two tubes of mascara, powder, and aspirin. There was also an address book which Clark put to one side. As he continued looking, he found a dial pack of birth control pills and a dozen condoms.

Miss Finch sniffed. "I hope, Doctor, that this will remain in your confidence."

"Of course," Clark said. Privately, he wondered about a girl who needed both condoms and pills.

Further search unearthed three canceled checks, a card for a beauty appointment six months ago, an old telephone bill, and an assortment of ticket stubs to theaters and movies.

"She's always been fond of movies," Miss Finch said. "She sees them all, even the ones she's not in."

Clark nodded, and continued rummaging. He found a final object: a small clear plastic cylinder with a flexible plastic top. It looked for all the world like a container for prescription pills, except for the size: it could not have held more than a single capsule. He turned it over in his hand.

"What's this?"

"I've never seen it before."

"Are you sure?"

"Yes. Sure."

Clark frowned. "It's obviously some kind of container . . ." He removed the top, and sniffed. He smelled nothing.

The purse was now empty. He turned it upside down and shook it, just to be sure. Something fell out with a metallic clang, struck the table, and bounced to the floor. He bent over to pick it up.

It was a small tuning fork.

"And this?"

"I don't know," Miss Finch said. "But I do know that one

of her dates gave it to her. She knew a lot of scientists and egghead types, you might say. They were always giving her things. One once gave her a telescope so she could look at the planets. She was always very interested in astrology."

Clark turned the fork over, examining the surfaces. There were no manufacturer's marks; he had never seen one like it before. He struck the tines against the table, and listened to the high-pitched hum. Then he shrugged, and dropped it back into the purse. He put the rest of the contents back in, except for the address book.

"I'd like to look through this."

"I really don't think that's a good idea," Miss Finch said. She took the address book and put it in the purse.

Harry, the intern, stuck his head into the conference room.

"I called all the people. The internist says he hasn't seen her for a year, and didn't prescribe anything. The psychiatrist is a real weirdo. Says he never prescribes drugs. The dermatologist is in Europe. And I checked on this Dr. George K. Washington."

"What about him?"

"He's not listed as an MD. There's a G.K. Washington in the phone book, but not as a doctor."

"She always called him Doctor," Miss Finch said.

"It is a little funny," Harry said.

"What's that?"

"Well, he lists an office and home phone. Here." He handed Clark the list of names and numbers.

"Maybe he's not a medical doctor," Clark said. Then he looked at the numbers more closely and frowned.

"Is something wrong?" Miss Finch said.

"No," Clark said. "Nothing at all."

He went again to check on Sharon Wilder, but her condition remained the same—stable, apparently sleeping, but unarousable. When he left the room, he met a short, powerfully built man in a black raw silk suit.

"How is she, Doc?"

"She appears all right."

The man held out his hand. "You're Clark, right? I'm Tony Lafora, Sharon's agent."

They shook hands. Lafora had a hearty grip. "You checked her over real good, Doc?"

"Yes, I did."

"Fine. Then I gotta talk to you."

"I'd like to talk to you, too."

At one end of the EW was a coffee machine. They went and got two cups, and took them back to the conference room. When they were alone, Lafora produced a hip flask and poured a shot into the coffee. He raised the cup in silent toast, gulped it back, and shivered.

"Now then, Doc. Give it to me straight. Is she gonna make it?"

"I think so."

"Look, Doc I'm strong. I'm tough. If she's—"

Clark said, "Your investment is secure, Mr. Lafora."

For a moment, Tony Lafora frowned, and then he smiled. "You mean it?"

"Well," Clark said, "we don't know what she took that made her unconscious. You may be able to help us with that. Do you know if she was taking any drugs?"

"Sharon?" He laughed. "Doc, she's had them all."

"How do you mean?"

"Well, she's an LA girl. Been around the town a long time. This is a drug town, all kinds of drugs."

"Was she taking any unusual drugs, anything experimental?"

Lafora shook his head. "No, nothing like that. Besides, don't want to do the drug thing on her. It won't work."

"It won't?"

"You know, it doesn't play right. It just doesn't *go*."

Clark said, "I don't understand."

"What I mean is, Sharon's a big star, and when a big star gets sick, there has to be an explanation for the press. Weirdo drugs don't work. The people in Des Moines don't buy it: how about phenobarb? Something simple?"

"It doesn't look like barbiturate intoxication."

"But you can't be positive, right?"

"No, we can't be *positive*, but—"

"Okay, Doc. Look: this is Thursday afternoon. We want to have something for the Friday papers, right? Let me work on it."

Clark said nothing. Lafora grabbed his hand and shook it.

"I knew I could count on you, Doc."

He gave Clark a slap on the back and was gone.

An hour later, when Clark went out to tell the press there was no change in Sharon's condition, he arrived to hear Tony Lafora telling them about the star's depression over a secret and very unhappy love, and how the star had probably taken phenobarb.

At six in the morning, a nurse called him to say that Sharon Wilder was awake.

He found her sitting up in the bed, clutching the sheet to her neck, looking very vulnerable, confused, and pretty.

"They tell me you saved my life," she said. Her voice was husky.

"Not really," he said.

"I want you to know I appreciate it."

"Any time," he said. He was struck by her beauty. She stared at him.

"You're kind of cute," she said.

He grinned. "So are you."

"Yeah, but I'm paid for it. Can I get dressed?"

"I think so. How do you feel?"

"Just great." She gave him a dazzling smile.

He found her clothes for her and waited outside while she dressed. When he returned, she was slipping into a pair of heels. He went over to the bed to look for the blue spot.

It was gone.

"Tell me, Miss Wilder—"

"Call me Sharon."

"All right, Sharon. What do you remember about yesterday evening?"

"Well, I got dressed early, because it was a new dress and I was afraid it wouldn't fit. So I took a shower, and dressed early, and did my face, and then sat down on the bed to relax before George arrived."

"George?"

"George Washington. He's this *adorable* biophysicist I know, really a dear. I don't know him very well, I just met him in fact."

"I see."

"And I was waiting for him to arrive."

"And?"

"And that's all I remember."

"Nothing else?"

She shook her head.

"Did you take anything?"

"A shower."

"I meant, any drugs?"

"No. Why?"

"We can't understand why you went into a coma."

She laughed. "Neither can I, but it doesn't matter, does it?" She kissed him on the cheek. "You're sweet to care. By the way, is there a phone around here?"

"In the hall."

"Good."

She went outside. Clark watched her go, unable to help noticing her body. He heard her drop a dime into the phone, and he thought about what she had said. He reached into his pocket and withdrew the list of physicians and their phone numbers that Harry had given him. It was rather odd that she claimed she didn't know George Washington well, he thought.

Because he had noticed a telephone bill in her purse. It was a bill three months old, and there were numerous long-distance charges to a number in Santa Monica.

The number was the office phone of George K. Washington. Odd.

He found himself listening to her conversation on the phone.

"Harvey? Listen, it was beautiful! Just beautiful! Scrambled my brains. Wow! Yes . . . I'll talk to you later. No, no problems at all. I think it's working. Fine. Right. Bye . . ."

She hung up.

Clark went out to sign her discharge papers. It was a brief formality, and afterward she shook hands with him and said, "Why don't you walk me out to my taxi?"

"All right."

On the way, she said, "You really are cute. I was watching you sign the forms. When are you coming over for a drink?"

"I'm pretty busy, Miss Wilder."

"I told you, call me Sharon." She smiled. "And even busy doctors get some time off."

Outside the hospital, he was surprised to find a half-dozen photographers. Sharon forced him to pose with her, and they took several more pictures as he helped her into the cab.

She looked out the window and said, "Remember that drink. My bar is always open and waiting."

Then she reached up and kissed him.

The flashbulbs popped.

3
TAILSPIN II

He was tired when he got home. The apartment, as usual, was a mess; he never seemed able to get it completely clean, even when a girl was coming over.

He pushed a pair of dirty socks off the couch and sat down to read his mail. There were bills for the most part; a letter from a friend in the army, saying he hated it; a note from his travel agent reporting that Clark's tickets to Mexico City were waiting, and that hotel reservations had been confirmed.

Clark was due for a month's vacation, to start in a week. He had been looking forward to a trip to Mexico, a chance to get away from California and everyone he knew, a chance to be by himself.

Now, he suddenly found the prospect of a month alone in Mexico City less agreeable. It surprised him to find he was thinking differently, and it was several minutes before he realized what had changed.

Sharon Wilder.

As soon as he thought of it, he pushed her from his mind. It was foolish to even contemplate; film people were terrible, demanding, petty and childish; he shouldn't even consider getting mixed up with . . .

He sighed.

He got up and made himself a drink, and then decided that he would call her, that it couldn't possibly hurt anything if he just *called*.

Sharon's number was not listed, so he called Gertrude Finch and got it from her.

A stiffly formal male voice answered: "Miss Wilder's residence."

"This is Dr. Clark calling. I wonder—"

"Oh yes, Dr. Clark. Miss Wilder left a message for you."

He had a queer sensation, part pleasure, part something else. "She did?"

"Yes, sir. I'll get it for you."

There was a pause, and then: "Dr. Clark? Pier Four, Marina Capitan. That's in Long Beach. You're to arrive after nine."

Clark frowned.

"Shall I repeat that, sir?"

"No," he said, still frowning.

"Very good, sir. Thank you for calling."

The man at the other end hung up.

"What do you know about that?" Roger Clark said aloud. And he decided that he knew nothing about that, and went to shower and change.

Marina Capitan was an elegant, exclusive mooring filled with huge powerboats. At night the boats, all polished wood and gleaming chrome, rocked quietly in the dark. On pier Four, a large cruiser was lighted and noisy; Clark headed toward it.

As he approached he could see people dancing on the stern and on the foredeck, and inside, people packed tight, drinking, talking, laughing.

He climbed the gangway, noting the name neatly stenciled on the bow: TAILSPIN II. As he came aboard he met a short, stocky man in bathing trunks and a knitted blue shirt.

"Who're you?" the man said.

"Roger Clark."

"I don't know you," the man said.

"I'm looking for Miss Wilder."

"Oh yes," the man said. He smiled. "You're the sawbones." He stuck out his hand. "Glad to have you aboard. Always glad to have a doctor: we may need you, after the broken glass. My name's Pietro O'Hara."

"How do you do. What broken glass?"

"Oh," O'Hara said, "there isn't any yet but there will be. I know: I've given parties like this before."

"It's your boat?"

"Of course." He grinned. "Business expense, naturally. Couldn't manage it otherwise. Come on down and get yourself onto my accountant's ledgers, and have a drink." O'Hara squeezed through the crowd toward the bar, and Clark followed. The people were well-dressed, though rather garishly; the women were showing a lot of—

"Scotch?" O'Hara said.

"Please."

—back, breasts, and legs. He noticed several quite stunning.

"She won't be here for a while," O'Hara said.

"Who?"

"Sharon. She always comes late, so to speak." He gave a gurgling chuckle that seemed to well up from his intestines. "You interested in art?"

In the corner, a girl wore Day-Glo body paint and nothing else. "Yes."

"Good. I'm an artist. I'll show you some of my stuff. Do you like that particular piece?"

"What piece?" He looked away from the girl, back to O'Hara.

"Judy," O'Hara said. "Did her this afternoon. A particularly effective composition, I believe. I like the colors and lines."

"Yes," Clark said.

"That particular work of art is for sale," O'Hara said. "Two hundred dollars. A night. Come along, and I'll show you some of my other things."

They pushed through the crowd until they came to a corner of the cabin. There they paused before a square block of wood, into which was set a four-foot piece of round doweling, with a pointed tip. On the doweling was a sign which said, HOSTILITY.

O'Hara beamed proudly. "How do you like it?"

"Remarkable," Clark said, taking a sip of Scotch.

"I'm very pleased with it. Came to me in a burst, a pure flash of inspiration. I was sleeping at the time, and jumped right up and built it."

"Very interesting."

"It's entitled, 'Hostility on Your Part.' That's because it's supposed to represent a phallus. Did you get that? Some people don't, right off."

Clark smiled.

"I think it's pretty funny, myself," O'Hara said, and laughed.

Clark laughed.

"Love a man with a sense of humor," O'Hara said. "Come on."

In another part of the room was a small wooden statue of a beaver. It was quite carefully and accurately made.

"Like it?"

"Very good."

"I call it 'The Ultimate Beaver.'"

O'Hara slapped his thigh, roared, and spilled his drink. Clark dutifully laughed.

"You can see the kind of a mind I have," O'Hara said, "but what the hell. I love my work. Come on."

Shortly, they came to a painting of a hamburger, rendered accurate in every detail. Catsup was oozing out of the sides of the bun. O'Hara paused to look critically at the painting for several minutes.

"Now then," he said, "this is a major work. Major."

"I see."

"Perhaps you can help me with it."

"I'll try."

"I finished this a year ago, and I haven't been able to decide on a title. No title, no money. Who'd buy a hamburger without a title?"

"Ummm."

"My first thought was 'Eat Me,' but that seemed a little obvious, don't you think?"

"Yes. Obvious."

"So then I thought of 'Meat Between Your Buns,' but that seemed a little gross."

"Gross," Clark nodded.

"You realize, of course, that my subject, my life's work, is filth. The future of pop art is filth and pornography. I'm trying to satirize pornography in my creations. See?"

"Yes."

"So if the title isn't good, it doesn't go. Listen, I'll tell you something. My first important piece, the one that brought me into the big time, was a thing I sold to some producer. It was an ordinary household fan, spray-painted shocking pink. You know what I called it?"

Clark shook his head, afraid to guess.

"'Blowjob,'" O'Hara announced in triumph. "That's what I called it, and it went for a thousand dollars. I had lots of offers for it. A great success. And now look at me." He waved his hand around the yacht. "I have money, women, fame, and fortune."

"I can see that."

O'Hara leaned close, and looked steadily at Clark. "Yeah, but I'll tell you. Man to man: I'm not happy."

"No?"

"It's true. I was happier when I was working as a garage mechanic, and dreaming of making it big. Now . . . success seems empty to me."

"I'm sorry to hear that," Clark said.

"It's the price of creativity," O'Hara said, and wandered off.

"Brilliant, absolutely brilliant," the man said. "If I say so myself. You know how it happened?"

"No," Clark said. He had begun speaking to the man a few minutes before; he had introduced himself as Johnny Kane. He was very drunk.

"Well, it was a beautiful spring day, and I was sitting in my office, thinking about the account. We needed a fresh approach, but we were limited. I mean, there are things you just can't say, and the public is sensitive. You can't have somebody say, 'My hemorrhoids were killing me, until I switched to X,' and you can't say, 'Boy, did I ever have trouble with cramps and farting until I discovered Y.' I'm talking about the *tracts*, now."

"I see," Clark said.

"So I was thinking, what do you say? What can you say? And then I realized that this was *deep down* distress, nothing shallow, but *deep down* distress, in the lower tract. For that deep down pain and discomfort in the lower tract, take the one medication that doctors recommend for their own—"

"Hello, darling," a voice whispered in his ear. He turned: Sharon was wearing a crochet dress over a bodystocking, and a calm smile. She looked directly at him.

"I hear there's a great view from the bridge," she said.

"Is there?"

"You mustn't miss it," she said.

She took his arm and they moved through the crowd, then up a narrow stairs. She went first; he followed.

"Stop looking at my legs," she said, as they went up.

"Be careful," he said, "or I'll bite your ankle."

She stopped.

She lifted her foot back, to his face.

He looked at it for a moment, then bit the ankle. It was rather pleasant, actually, salty and nice.

She laughed. "Does that appeal to you?"

"No. It's the way I get my kicks. Lost two front teeth once."

"I'll remember to be careful," she said, and laughed again.

Up on the bridge, they could look down on the foredeck, and the couples dancing in the moonlight.

"I was afraid you wouldn't telephone," she said. "But I'm glad you decided to come."

"Anytime," he said.

"Well, later then," she said.

"Ladies first," he said.

She laughed. "My, you doctors are daring on your nights off."

And he looked at her, and he thought to himself that it was

funny, it was all pretty funny, and the drink was hitting him awfully hard, and Sharon said "I like considerate men," and he moved forward to kiss her.

And fell. A long, long way.

4
THE LOVE NEXT

"Rise and shine."

He opened his eyes and smelled coffee. Sunlight streaming into a large room, across a vast bed. Sheets touching his skin. Sharon Wilder standing over him in a short robe, holding a tray.

"Good morning," she said. "Did you sleep well?" He was confused, still thinking oddly and slowly. The boat . . .

"Very well."

"Good," she said. She set the tray on the bed and stretched. "So did I."

He looked across the bed at the other pillow, and then he looked back at her. She wore no makeup, her hair was loose and tangled, and she looked marvelous.

She handed him a coffee cup. "I hope you don't mind," she said, "about last night."

"Not a bit," he said, trying to remember.

"I know it must have been dull for you," she said.

He had a vague memory, a slight stirring. "Absolutely not. It was wonderful."

"I meant the party," she said. "That dreadful party."

"Oh yes."

She giggled and kissed him on the neck. His coffee spilled; he jumped; she giggled again.

"I like you," she said.

Then she went into a large closet, and began to dress. He glanced around the room. It was done in gold and white, with a huge bed covered with a canopy.

"Is this your bedroom?"

She giggled. "Yes. Don't you remember?"

He looked out the window, at a broad lawn. "And your house?"

"Yes. I call it the Love Nest. Do you like it?"

"Well, I haven't seen very much of it."

"Silly, I showed it all to you last night."

"I meant the house."

"So did I."

She came out wearing a short skirt and blouse. "You'll probably want to take a shower. It's right in there." She pointed to a door.

"Thanks."

"Meantime I'll make breakfast. Eggs and bacon?"

"You cook too?"

"Just mornings. I don't like the servants around in the mornings."

She walked out of the room and he got slowly up from the bed. He could remember nothing of the night before, nothing since being on the bridge of the boat.

It was odd, disorienting. He must have been drunk as hell. Yet there was no hangover; in fact, he felt marvelous. Better than he'd felt in a long time.

He walked around the room, looking at her makeup desk, her closet, a small writing table in the corner. There was a letter on top of the desk; he glanced at it curiously. It was from a travel agency, stating that her two tickets to San Cristobal Island were enclosed. The payment had been made by Advance, Inc. and all was in order. She would fly by jet from Los Angeles to Miami, and change planes for Nassau. From there she would travel by the special hotel airplane to San Cristobal.

Clark frowned. He had never heard of San Cristobal. And he wondered about the hotel; the letter did not specify it by name.

Peculiar, he thought.

He stepped into the shower and turned it on, very hot.

———

When he came out, he began to look for his clothes. They were not in the bedroom; he looked out in the hall and found a tie and a pair of socks. He picked them up and continued, finding his shirt, then his pants. He came into a living room, very simple and elegant. His jacket was thrown over a couch, his shoes on the floor, and two half-finished martinis stood on the coffee table.

"Find everything?" Sharon called.

"Yes, thanks."

He dressed and went into the kitchen. Sharon was scooping eggs onto two plates. He sat down and they ate; she was in a hurry: she had a beauty parlor appointment in an hour, and then the photographers an hour after that . . .

He smiled. "Busy girl."

"Not really. Just pre-publicity for the next film. Actually, I'm going on vacation in a week."

"That's funny. So am I."

"Where are you going?"

"Mexico City."

She made a face. "Don't like it," she said. "Too dusty. You should go where I'm going."

"Where's that?"

"San Cristobal. It's a new resort in the Caribbean."

That explained why he had never heard of it. On an impulse, he said, "Why don't we go together?"

She shook her head. "Can't."

"Why not?"

She gave him an odd smile. "Previous engagement. Maybe next vacation?"

"All right," he said. "Maybe the next one."

5
SHINE ON

He took a cab back to the Long Beach pier, got into his car, sat down, and thought things over. He was feeling suddenly very peculiar. He had just spent the night with Sharon Wilder—every man's dream—and he could remember nothing about it. He had slept in her bed, showered in her shower, eaten breakfast in her kitchen, and God knew what else.

And he could remember nothing about it

Today was his day off, and he had intended to spend it with the travel agent, discussing his vacation plans. But he was puzzled, feeling off-balance. Reaching into his pocket, he found the list of doctors Sharon Wilder had been seeing. An internist, a dermatologist, a psychiatrist, and the mysterious Dr. George K. Washington.

He decided, for no very good reason, to pay a call on the psychiatrist.

Dr. Abraham Shine seemed to own two houses. One was located near the road, a modern, rectangular structure. There was a sign by the door which said, "Office." Farther back, along a gravel drive, was a mansion of pink stucco, secluded among carefully tended shrubs and bushes. Clark parked and went into the office.

He immediately found himself in a small but plush reception area. Two things attracted his attention. There was a massive modern structure sculpture of interlocking polished chrome spheres. And there was a receptionist with large eyes and spheres that did not interlock.

"May I help you?"

"I'm, uh, Dr. Clark, Roger Clark . . ."

"Yes, Doctor. Do you have an appointment?"

"Well, no—"

"I'm afraid it's necessary to make an appointment to see the doctor."

"Actually, I just wanted to see him for a few minutes—"

The receptionist shook her head. Other things moved as well. "I'm sorry, Dr. Shine is very firm. You must have an appointment to see him. After all," she said, in a reasonable voice, "if he took people without an appointment, where would we be?"

Clark was thinking that over when she said, "I can't tell you how many people—sick, troubled people like yourself—have come to us and asked to see the doctor for just a few minutes. He has to keep his schedule. Think of all the suffering, the unhappiness, the sad and lost souls that we treat here."

"In Beverly Hills?"

"Rich people," the girl said sternly, "are not necessarily happy people."

Somehow, the way she said it, Clark had the feeling she was quoting somebody. He had an idea who it might be.

"Look, Miss—"

"Connor. Janice Connor."

"Look, Miss Connor, I'm not seeking advice for myself."

"A relative? Your wife?"

"No, I'm not married."

"I see," she said. She began to smile at him.

"Actually, Miss Connor, this is a professional matter concerning a mutual patient of Dr. Shine and myself."

"Well..."

"And Miss Connor, I know this may be impertinent of me, but..."

"Yes..."

"Are you free for dinner?"

"Yes," she said.

"Eight o'clock?"

"Yes," she said.

"And about seeing Dr. Shine..."

"He has a free half-hour," she said, "at ten-thirty."

The office was large, furnished as plushly as a bordello. Clark entered to see Dr. Abraham Shine rising from behind his desk.

"Dr. Clark, is it?" Shine said.

"Yes." Clark looked at Shine. It was a shock to see how old the man was. His face was heavily creased, his hair white and thin, his body paunchy.

"I'm from LA Memorial."

"Oh, yes. One of your people called me about Sharon Wilder, if I remember."

"That's right."

"Well, I have a free half hour. If you don't mind sitting by the pool, we can talk there."

"Of course."

They went through a rear door, and walked up the grassy lawn toward the mansion. Shine led him around to the back, toward a large swimming pool. Shine dropped into a deck chair and motioned Clark to another alongside.

"Time was," he said, "when I'd use these half-hour breaks to swim. Madly: five miles a day. Now, I couldn't get from one end of that pool to the other." He sighed. "I'm seventy-two years old, and feeling every minute of it."

Shine shook his head, and stared at the water. There was a moment of silence; Clark waited, then said, "About Sharon Wilder..."

"Oh yes. Sharon. Remarkable young woman. She'll go far, I think. Very far, in this town. When she came to me, of course, she was rather upset."

"How so?"

"Well, she was just beginning her, ah, campaign to appear on the cover of everything published in the western world. She is a sensitive girl, and she was bothered by a recurrent delusion."

"Oh?"

"Yes. She was convinced that she was just a pawn, an instrument being manipulated by some shadowy organization."

Clark thought of Tony Lafora. "But her agent is—"

"Not her agent," Shine said. "It had nothing to do with her agent. She was bothered by thoughts of some kind of giant, scientific corporation which was controlling her life and career. She dreamed about it."

"Very peculiar."

"Not really. It's a rather common delusion among young girls in this town. I suppose because it isn't really a delusion—for many of them, it's absolutely true. The studios manipulate them, humiliate them, exploit them, use them. And then discard them when they begin to show the wear and tear."

"What corporation was Sharon worried about?"

"She couldn't say. That was the trouble. She couldn't get that clear in her own mind. It was a sort of free-floating, American anxiety. Fear of the great corporation—"

"—in the sky."

Shine laughed. "I suppose. Anyway, I cured her of it by my usual method: hypnosis. My techniques are unorthodox, but they work. I put her into a deep trance, and then counter-suggested various ego-affective principles. After three sessions, she was convinced that her destiny was in her own hands, that she was free. That's not really true, of course, but it is an easier delusion to live with."

"I see," Clark said.

At that moment, a strikingly beautiful blonde girl appeared by the pool. She could not have been more than eighteen or nineteen, and she wore a very small, very thin red bikini. "Your daughter?"

"My wife," Dr. Shine said, with a contented sigh.

The girl nodded to them, and dived into the pool. She swam back and forth with long, easy strokes. They watched for a while, then Clark said, "Did you prescribe any drugs for Sharon?"

"No. I do not believe in drugs. They are a waste of time. Psychoactive drugs depend heavily upon suggestion; every clinical study has proven that, beyond question. I prefer to give the suggestion directly, and skip the chemicals."

"Do you know if she was taking any drugs from other sources?"

"Yes. Certainly she was. Her sexual frustrations were driving her to seek satisfactions in other areas. At one time I was afraid she would become a narcotics addict, but that never happened, fortunately."

"Did she talk much about drugs?"

"Only in the beginning. They fascinated her: part of her preoccupation with manipulation and artificial personalities, supplied from some external source. She believed, for a time, that drugs could really change her, make her something else, something different. I was able to correct that attitude."

"What is your opinion of her present status?"

"Sharon's? Excellent. One of my most successful cases."

Clark nodded politely. He was obviously getting nowhere. He stood, thanked Dr. Shine for his time, and was about to leave when a thought occurred to him.

"By the way," he said, "have you ever treated any Angels?"

"Angels?"

"Hell's Angels."

"Funny you should ask. I have one under treatment now."

"Who's that?"

"Arthur Lewis. A wild one. His father's a television producer, and there is a lot of money. The boy's assimilating it badly. Victim of affluence, you might say. Why do you ask?"

"Just wondered," Clark said.

Ten minutes later, after Clark had gone, Mrs. Shine climbed out of the pool and toweled herself dry.

"Who was that?" she asked her husband.

"A doctor. He's been treating some of the coma people, and I'm afraid he's puzzled. He didn't come out and say it, but it was on his mind."

"What are you going to do about it?"

"Nothing. Nothing at all," Dr. Shine said, smiling.

"You mean he's—"

"Exactly. He's the one."

"Poor guy. He was kind of cute."

"Don't worry," Shine said. "He'll be well taken care of."

6
INTERLUDE: SYBOCYL

Returning to his apartment, Clark found Peter Moss in the lobby. Moss was the detail man for Wilson, Speck, and Loeb, the drug company. As usual, he carried a huge satchel stuffed with samples.

"Hello, Roger. I was just calling to see if you were home."

"Come on up," Clark said.

They rode the elevator together. "Got some great new stuff this time," Moss said, patting the satchel. "Great new stuff."

"What is it this month? Antihypertensives?" There had recently been a spate of new antihypertensive drugs from several companies. The detail men were pushing them like mad.

"Naw. That's old stuff. Now we're working with Sybocyl."

The elevator arrived at the tenth floor. Clark unlocked the door to his apartment. "Sybocyl? What's that?"

"New stuff, just finished clinical testing. The FDA is going to release it in about a week."

"Yes; but what is it?"

"Marvelous stuff," Moss said, sitting down and opening his briefcase.

Clark took off his jacket and tie. "Yes, but what?"

"The FDA is just finishing up on it. Testing the rats and monkeys. For a while, we didn't think we could market it, because it caused toxic reactions in the yellow ostrich."

"Really?"

"Yes. Seems it drove them insane. Lost all desire to bury their heads in sand. Of course, it only affected *female* ostriches."

"Who discovered this?"

"The FDA. They also discovered that it turned the second molars of immature Hamadryas baboons an odd brown color. That was a setback, too."

"I'm sure. But what about people?"

"Well, you know how it is. With such odd reactions in animals, the FDA was unwilling to release it for clinical trial. And after the business with the Norway rat—"

"What was that?"

"Well, they discovered that administration of the drug to the Norway rat, research strain K-23, induced uncontrollable vomiting."

"Unfortunate," Clark said.

"A mechanism involving the chemoreceptor trigger zone in the medulla was postulated."

"Quite naturally."

"Well, no," Moss said. "After all, there might have been a peripheral effect as well as a central one."

"Yes," Clark admitted. He had learned long ago that you had to let Moss talk for a while. Like most detail men, Moss had attended a junior college in business administration; he knew nothing about science or drugs, but had read the journals and dutifully memorized them.

"Of course," Moss continued, "there was one hitch. In order to induce the vomiting, they had to administer rather heavy doses."

"Oh?"

"In fact, they had to administer the rat's own weight in the drug."

"I see."

"Hardly a physiologic condition. After all, can you imagine giving a 150-pound man 150 pounds of penicillin? Make anyone sick. Still, the FDA was suspicious. It was months," Moss said, "before we started the clinical trials. They were done in Baltimore, Chicago, and Cleveland, and fortunately, responses were gratifying. Sybocyl passed with flying colors." Moss reached into his satchel and produced a small bottle of pink capsules. "And here it is!" he cried dramatically, thrusting it into Clark's hands.

"Very nice," Clark said, looking at the bottle.

"Sybocyl," said Moss, "is the ultimate wonder drug. It stops cardiac arrhythmias, is a bronchodilator, has direct diuretic effects, stimulates the myocardium to increase contractility, is bactericidal, and is a CNS stimulant and sedative."

"A stimulant and sedative?"

"Strange as it seems," Moss said, "it is. The ultimate wonder drug. You can give it for anything except measles and clap."

"Remarkable," Clark said, frowning. "Any side effects?"

"None."

"None?"

"None at all." Moss chuckled. "It has so many therapeutic effects, there's hardly room for side effects, eh?"

"What about contraindications?" Contraindications were medical situations in which the drug could not be given.

"Relatively few. There are one or two."

"What are they?"

"Here," Moss said. "I'll give you the literature." He stood and looked at his watch. "Time for me to be off. Can I leave anything else with you?"

"Some aspirin," Clark said. "I have a headache."

Moss frowned. "We have something much better than aspirin. Have you tried Phenimol?"

"No."

"Great stuff. Antipyretic, anti-inflammatory, and very strong analgesic. No side effects. And it works very well on cancer of the colon, if you happen to have—"

"I don't."

"Well, it's just great for headaches. Just great."

"Addicting?"

"Well, yes . . ."

"I'll take the aspirin," Clark said.

Moss gave it to him regretfully. As he was leaving, Clark said, "By the way, Pete. You keep up with the experimental drugs, don't you?"

"Well, I try."

"Heard anything about a drug that changes urine color?"

"Changes it how?"

"Turns it blue."

"Blue? No. Why?"

"How about a drug that puts you into a coma?"

Moss laughed. "I can't imagine a market for it."

"Neither can I," Clark said. But the joke started him thinking: suppose Sharon Wilder and Arthur Lewis hadn't taken the drug accidentally. Suppose they had taken it for a purpose, a specific reason, and the coma was an unrelated side effect . . .

He shook his head. He didn't even know that Sharon or the Angel had taken a drug.

After Peter Moss had gone, Clark picked up the bottle of Sybocyl and read the sheet of effects, indications, and contraindications:

Contraindications: Sybocyl should not be used with diabetics, hypertensives, pregnant women, males over forty, infants, children, adolescents, or persons with myopia or dental caries. The drug may otherwise be prescribed with absolute safety.

"Great stuff," Clark said. He crumpled the sheet and took the bottle into the bathroom. He poured the pills down the toilet and flushed it, watching as the pink capsules swirled, and were gone.

7
ADVANCE, INC.

He sat in his apartment and thought over what had happened to him. He decided that it had all been very peculiar, and very unenlightening. He could, of course, make further calls; he could check with Sharon Wilder's other doctors, and with George K. Washington, whoever he was. But he had the strange feeling that nothing would come of it, and meantime, there was his Mexico trip to plan for. He was about to call his travel agent when the phone rang.

It was Harry, the intern. "Listen, Rog, I thought you'd want to know. Andrews, the Chief of Medicine, just called. Wanted to know about people urinating blue."

"Oh?"

"Yes. I told him about the two cases you had, and described them."

"And?"

"And he thanked me and hung up."

"No explanation?"

"None. But I wouldn't be surprised if he called you later."

"Okay," Clark said. "Thanks."

As soon as he hung up, the phone rang again.

"Dr. Clark speaking."

"Clark, this is George Andrews."

"Hello, Dr. Andrews."

"Clark, I'm calling about some patients you've seen. An Angel named Arthur Lewis, alias Little Jesus, and—"

"Sharon Wilder."

"Yes. That's right." Andrews seemed surprised. "How did you know?"

"They were the same kind of patient."

"That's what I wanted to speak to you about. As I understand it, they presented with coma, no localizing signs, no respiratory or cardiac depression, and no after-effects when they recovered. Is that right?"

"Yes sir."

"And they both urinated blue?"

"Yes sir."

"The reason I ask," Andrews said, "is that I just got a call from Murdoch at San Francisco General. They get a lot of the Berkeley drug abusers, as well as the Hashbury loonies. Yesterday they got five people in coma as the result of a police raid. General didn't know what to do about them, so they waited, and the people all came out of it. And there was this blue urine business as well. Murdoch wanted to know if we'd had any similar experience."

Clark frowned. "He had five cases?"

"Five. Everybody up there is terrified of more. Murdoch's convinced a new kind of drug is going around. They don't know where it's coming from, or who's making it, or what the chemical nature is like. And the kids aren't talking, when they come out of the coma. They claim they don't remember."

"Perhaps they don't," Clark said.

"Exactly," Andrews said. "There may be a retroactive

amnesia. Clark, this could be a serious problem. Very serious. Have you investigated your two patients at all?"

"As a matter of fact, sir, I have. I suspected a new drug, and I've looked into their history of ingestion as carefully as I could. I spent the morning with Sharon Wilder's doctors—"

"Good man."

"—and came up with nothing."

Andrews sighed. "Very serious problem," he repeated. "I can't urge you strongly enough to follow it up. You know," he said, "you and I must have a little talk soon."

"Sir?"

"Well, the hospital has to decide on a chief resident for next year."

"Yes, sir."

"This drug thing is a very serious problem, very serious indeed. Anyone who clears it up will be doing a great service to the medical community. An immense service. As I recall, you're going on vacation soon."

"Yes, sir."

"Have a good time," Andrews said. "I'll talk to you when you get back." And he hung up.

Clark stared at the telephone for several minutes, and then said aloud, "I've been bribed."

He rummaged through his notebook and came up with the list of Sharon Wilder's physicians. At the bottom of the list was George K. Washington. Office number: 754–6700, extension 126.

He dialed it. After a moment, a pleasant female voice said, "Advance, Incorporated. Good afternoon."

"Extension one two six, please."

"One moment, please."

There was a click as the switchboard put him through. Then more ringing, and another woman's voice.

"Dr. Washington's office."

"This is Dr. Clark calling from LA Mem—"

"Oh yes, Dr. Clark."

Clark stopped. Oh yes?

"We've been waiting for your call," the girl said. "Dr. Washington is in conference now, but he asked me to tell you an appointment has been set up for four this afternoon. You can discuss the job with him at that time."

"The job?"

"Yes. You *are* applying for a job, aren't you?"

"Uh . . . yes."

"We'll see you then, Doctor."

Clark hesitated. There was obviously some mistake, but he might as well take advantage of it.

"One question," he said. "How do I get there?"

"Take the Santa Monica Freeway to the Los Calos exit, then go north a quarter of a mile. You can't miss it. There's a black sign that says Advance, Incorporated by the road."

Clark hung up and scratched his head. He thought about the name of the corporation; it seemed very familiar. But he could not remember where he had heard it before. After several minutes, he put his tie back on, slipped into his jacket, and headed for the parking lot.

The secretary had been right. It was impossible to miss the sign. It was constructed of black stone, with white lettering:

ADVANCE INC.

BIOSYSTEMS SPECIALISTS

He turned off the road, and parked in a lot alongside the main building, which was starkly modern, with walls of green glass. The building was two stories high, and about as large as any of a dozen other small, specialized scientific firms around Los Angeles. In recent years, attracted by government contracts and good weather, scientists had flocked to Southern California, which now had a greater number and higher concentration of scientific minds than any other place in the history of the world.

He paused to look at the building, and wondered what went on inside. He couldn't tell; it might have been anything from electronics to political science research. He went through the large glass doors to the area marked "Reception." A woman looked up.

"Can I help you?"

"My name is Clark. I have an appointment with Dr. Washington."

"Yes, sir."

She telephoned, spoke briefly, then turned to Clark.

"If you'll just have a seat, please."

Clark sat down on a Barcelona chair in the corner, and thumbed through an issue of *The American Journal of Parapsychology* while he waited. In a few minutes, a heavyset guard appeared.

"Dr. Clark?"

"Yes."

"Please come with me."

Clark followed the guard down a corridor. They stopped at a nearby room. An old woman was there, surrounded by electronic equipment.

"He's to see Dr. Washington," the guard explained.

"All right," said the woman. She nodded to a camera. "Look over there."

Clark looked. Out of the corner of his eye, he saw her press a button; the camera clicked.

"State your name loudly and clearly for our voice recorders."

"Doctor Roger Clark."

"No, no," the woman said. "That will never do. Just your *name*."

"Roger Clark," he said.

"Thank you," the woman said. She produced a form. "Sign here, please. Waiver of liability."

"Waiver?"

"It's routine. Do you want to see Dr. Washington, or not?"

Clark signed. It was all so peculiar, he did not want to argue.

"Thank you," the woman said, and looked down at her desk.

Clark went on, following the guard, to an elevator. As they walked down the corridor, Clark glanced at the doors, with their neatly stenciled markings:

ALPHA WAVE SYNCH LAB
MASSACT RES UNIT
K PUPPIES
HYPNOESIS 17
WHITE ENVIRON

Clark said, "What kind of work is done here?"

"All kinds," the guard said.

They got into the elevator and went to the second floor. The guard led him down another corridor to a door marked ENERGICS SUBGROUP. He opened it, and waved Clark inside.

A secretary sat typing a letter, wearing earphones attached to a dictaphone machine. She turned off the machine and removed the earphones. "Dr. Clark? Dr. Washington is expecting you." She pressed the intercom. "You may go right in."

Clark passed through a second door, into the sloppiest office he had ever seen. The walls were lined with shelves, which contained pamphlets, notebooks, and stacks of loose paper; books and journals sat in unruly heaps on the floor and on the desk. From behind the debris on the desk, a thin, pale figure rose.

"I am George Kelvin Washington. Do sit down."

Clark looked for a place to sit. There was a chair, but it was heaped high with manuscripts and journals.

"Just push that junk off," Dr. Washington said. "It's not important anyway. Make yourself comfortable."

Dr. Washington sank back down behind the stacks on the desk. A moment later, he cleared a little tunnel, which allowed him to see Clark, sitting in the chair.

"You've come about the job," Washington said.

"Yes, I—"

"Good, good. You seem a bright young man. I'm not surprised that your interest in Advance, Inc. has been aroused."

"Yes, it—"

"There is no question that you would find our work challenging. We operate at the very forefront of several areas of investigation. The very forefront."

"I see," Clark said, not seeing.

"If I understand correctly," Washington said, staring down at his desk, "you are a, ah, where is it, oh yes—you are a pharmacologist."

"That's correct," Clark said. He wondered how Washington knew. He wondered what Washington was looking at, on the desk.

"Your job application," Washington said, "is all in order. Quite complete. I needn't tell you that we are most interested in your experience in clinical drug testing at the National Institutes. You did that instead of military service?"

"Yes."

"Good. Excellent. And you've had some experience with human drug testing?"

"Limited."

"Ummm. How limited?"

"Well, we did several tests on experimental drugs for cancer—"

"Yes, yes, all that's down here," Washington said, tapping the sheet. "Cancer drugs numbered JJ-4225 and AL-19. Controlled double-blind clinical trials involving forty and sixty-nine subjects, respectively. Is that it?"

"Yes," Clark said, frowning. He had filled out no application. He had certainly never written down—

"Well, that's fine," Washington said. "Just fine. Undoubtedly you're curious about the work you will be doing, if you choose to join the team here."

"As a matter of fact, I am."

"You'll understand if I can't be too specific," Dr. Washington said, scratching the tip of his nose. "We are not a secret organization, but we do need to be careful."

"You do a lot of government work?"

"Heavens, no! We don't do any at all. We used to do government work, but that stage is past. Entirely past." Dr. Washington sighed. "Your work will concern the interaction of organ systems with chemical compounds which affect multiple bodily systems. In most cases, one of the systems will be nervous, but this will not be invariably so."

"This work is drug testing, then?"

"In a manner of speaking."

"I'm not sure I understand."

"Well," Washington said, "take my own work. I'm a biophysicist, myself. I've been working on stereochemical interactions of allosteric enzymes. Very challenging."

"I'm sure. What sort of—"

"Enzymes? Those affecting tryptophan metabolism. Effects upon thyroid, brain, and kidney . . . precisely the kind of multiple system situation I was describing."

Clark said, "Can you tell me a little more about the company itself?"

"Yes. We're a new company, just started two years ago. As you can see, we've grown enormously in that period. Advance has a total staff of 207, including fifty secretaries. We have nine divisions, each involved in some broad question of the application of science to man. We are working in electromagnetics, enzymes, ultrasound, peripheral perception. A wide variety of fields."

"Where do most of your contracts come from?"

"We are a private research and development firm. We make our services available to private industry. But mostly, we work for ourselves."

"For yourselves?"

"Yes. That is to say, we exploit our own developments. To that extent, we are unique among firms of this type. But I believe that we represent the way of the future—we are the R-and-D team of the future. Right here, right now. We do everything: we develop, we apply, and we exploit. Do you follow me?"

"I follow you," Clark said. In fact, he did not understand it at all.

"I'd like," said Washington, "for you to meet with our president, if you have the time. Better than anyone else, he can tell you about Advance, and what it stands for."

"That would be wonderful."

"Good. I'll try to arrange it."

He got up from behind his desk and went to the door. "I won't be a minute," he said and left, shutting the door behind him.

Clark was alone.

Immediately, he got up and went around behind the desk. He was looking for the paper that Washington had been reading from; Clark's application. But he did not find it. Indeed, behind the stack of books and pamphlets, the desk was bare.

He opened the drawer to the desk and looked inside. The first thing that he found was a small tuning fork, like the one in Sharon Wilder's purse.

The second thing was an odd sheet of paper:

WILDER, SHARON (ALICE BLANKFURT)

INDICES:

SYLONO	.443
PSYCHOSEXUAL	.387
LIENO	.003
DERMO-PHONIC	.904
CRYO	.342
HYPERSTHENIC	.887

SUMMARY: Initial work with this model reveals satisfactory assimilation of basic parameters with excellent prognosis for future interaction in K-K. There can be no doubt that—

He heard a noise outside, closed the drawer, and resumed his seat.

Dr. Washington returned. "Sorry about the delay," he said. "Dr. Blood will see you immediately, if that is convenient."

"Yes."

"Good."

He nodded to the door. "The guard will take you there." Washington extended his hand. "Good luck, Dr. Clark. I hope you'll be joining us."

"Thank you," Clark said.

———

Dr. Harvey Blood, president of Advance, Inc., had the largest desk Clark had ever seen. It was curved, bean-shaped, and nine feet long. The surface was brightly polished mahogany. Dr. Blood sat behind his desk, and his face was mirrored in the polish. Clark noticed that the surface was unmarred by pen, paper, or intercom.

"Well, well, well!" Dr. Blood stood, a stocky, red-faced cherub with black unruly hair. "So you're Dr. Clark."

"Yes, sir."

"Sit down, Clark. Roger, is it? Let me tell you something about our company, Roger."

Clark sat.

"I won't give you a sales pitch, Roger. I'll just give you the straight dope. We're a young company, and a growing company. We've been in existence for less than five years, and already you can see how we've grown. By the end of the year, we will employ more than three hundred people."

"Very impressive, sir."

"It certainly is," Blood said, with a smile. "But we're not stopping at three hundred. We're not stopping at three thousand. Far from it: we are going to expand *indefinitely*."

"Indefinitely?"

"Yes. Look here: what's the largest corporation in America today?"

Clark shrugged. "General Motors, I suppose."

"Right! And what does General Motors do?"

"Makes automobiles."

"Right again! And what is so great about making automobiles?"

"Well—"

"The answer," Harvey Blood said, "is that there is nothing very great about automobiles. They are a terrible product. They are destroying our landscape, ruining our cities, poisoning our air. Automobiles are the curse of the modern world."

"I suppose if you look at it—"

"I do, I do. But now I ask you: what could a corporation do, if it manufactured some product which was not destructive, ruinous, and poisonous? What limits would there be?"

"None."

"Exactly! None. And if that corporation went even further, to the point where it manufactured positive, healthful, beautiful products *and* instilled the desire for them, where would it all end?"

Clark said nothing.

"You see? You see how perfect it is?"

Clark could not understand how this was related to enzymes involved in tryptophan synthesis. He said so.

"Look here," Blood said. "We haven't got a use for tryptophan yet. But we're working on it. We're developing it. That's what we do here, develop things. We take raw, crude scientific innovation, and we produce applications for it. We innovate, we cogitate, we initiate—the three pillars of our advancing firm." He chuckled briefly. "You see, Roger, we are specialists in putting knowledge to use. We accumulate useless information, and make it useful. We innovate, cogitate, initiate."

"I see."

"And we pay extremely well. I don't know if you were told,

but starting salary for a person of your qualifications is 49,500 dollars."

"Very reasonable."

"A well-paid employee is a happy employee, Roger."

"Yes."

"I won't beat around the bush, Roger. You're thinking of working in our biochemical division, testing drugs. That is one of the most exciting divisions we have. Our people are engaged in testing and applying new compounds in ways previously undreamed of. We are working on the *frontiers of research*."

It occurred to Clark that he still had remarkably little idea about the company, and the job they were offering him.

"Intellectual stimulation, pleasant working conditions, and financial compensation. That is what we provide for our employees."

"Where exactly would I be working? In this building?"

"No," Blood said. "Our research facilities are located a short distance away. Naturally, since many of our projects are confidential, we must maintain a certain amount of secrecy."

"Yes."

Someone entered the room, a cheerful young man, carrying what looked like a large poster.

"I'm sorry, Dr. Blood, but we need approval of the dummy."

"All right," Blood said.

Clark leaned forward, hoping for a look at the poster. He could see that it was a penciled drawing of some kind, like an ad for something. Spaces for copy and photographs were blocked out.

Dr. Blood looked at it closely. "What's it for?"

"*The New Yorker*," the man said. "That's our first big market."

"All right," Dr. Blood said. "Go ahead with it."

"Thank you, sir," the man said, and left.

"Well now, Roger, where were we? Oh yes, talking about secrecy. It's a problem, Roger. I'll be frank. Our confidential work imposes restrictions on all of us. But we manage, and I'm sure you won't find it much of a burden." He looked at his watch. "Now, I'm afraid I must go. I have an, ah, appointment in half an hour. Do you have any other questions?"

"No, I don't think so."

"Fine. Then we'll expect to hear of your decision within the next few days."

"All right."

"Good luck, Roger."

Clark left, with a final glimpse of the stocky, red-faced man and his enormous polished desk. Harvey Blood smiled benignly.

Roger Clark smiled back.

8
THE PLACE TO GO

Aero Travel, located on the unfashionable (eastern) end of Sunset Strip, was operated by Ron Harmon. Clark had known him since college days; they had both been in the same fraternity. Since then, Clark had booked all his vacations through Aero and Harmon had arranged for discounts wherever possible. They were old friends.

Clark arrived at the office late in the day, just as Harmon was preparing to shut down. Clark went in, looking past the posters of Switzerland and Hawaii, and inquired about his reservations for Mexico.

"For what?" Harmon said. He seemed rather distant and preoccupied.

"Mexico. You remember."

"Mexico?" He searched among his files.

"Ron, are you feeling okay?"

"Yes, yes, I feel fine." Harmon continued to search. His fingers moved slowly, sluggishly through the stacks of papers in his desk drawer.

"You aren't acting fine."

"What? Oh. Listen, I just got back."

"Back?"

"Listen," Harmon said, ignoring the files and closing the drawer. "Listen, Roger, you don't want to go to Mexico."

"I don't?"

"Hell no. Listen, I just got back."

"Back from what?"

Harmon sighed. "That's a good question. It's really back from *where*, but it doesn't matter. Back from *what* is just as good."

Clark said nothing.

"Listen, Roger, I'm your buddy, right?"

"Right."

"And I'm a travel agent, right?"

"Right."

"So listen: will you take my advice?"

Clark hesitated. "That depends."

"Don't go to Mexico, Roger."

"Why?"

"Don't go." Harmon stared at him, his eyes distant. "Don't go."

"But Ron, I thought it was all set up, the plane reservations, the hotels . . ."

"It is. But don't go."

"Didn't you tell me that the girls in Mexico City were—"

"Forget that. I've learned my lesson."

"What lesson?"

"Listen," Ron Harmon said "I just got back from the greatest place in the world. It's a new resort, it's just fabulous, and in a year or so it will be the most famous vacation spot in the world, bar none. As a tourist attraction, it's unsurpassed. It's better than the Alhambra in Spain, better than the pyramids in Egypt, better than the Taj Mahal in India, better than anything."

Clark said, "What is it?"

"It's great," Harmon said. "Absolutely great. Nothing can touch it for rest, relaxation, excitement, adventure—"

"But what is it?"

"It's a resort," Harmon said. "A brand-new resort of a type previously unknown. We're in the middle of an age, you know. The resort age. Travel is greater than ever before in history, and resorts are booming as never before. The Aga Khan is developing Sardinia. The Costa Brava is booming. South America is just beginning; the Caribbean is expanding fantastically. But all of these places offer basically the same thing—sun, a new environment, a little action . . ."

"So?"

"So once in a great while, a new thing comes along. Something *different*. Really different. And that has just happened."

"What has?"

"A new resort which is really new and different. Really exciting, really special. I've just been to this resort: they invited all the travel agents out there for a week, to see what it was like. I must tell you: it's the place to go."

"It is?"

"No question," Ron Harmon said. "No question about it. You'll have a fantastic time. I did."

"Where is this resort? What's it like?"

"It's on an island," Harmon said, "called San Cristobal."

Clark said nothing. He was feeling very peculiar, as if he had eaten something raw, and it was now disagreeing with his stomach.

"San Cristobal?"

"It's in the Caribbean," Ron said. "A brand-new island—not really, of course—but brand-new in the sense of development. It's been built up quietly by a group of Americans, to make it into the finest resort in the world. And they've succeeded."

"How do you mean?"

"This island," Ron Harmon said, "is about five square miles. It's mostly bare coral and scrubby trees, and vegetation. But it's been bought up, and modernized, and now . . ." He sighed. His eyes were staring off into space.

"And now?"

"Beautiful."

"What's it like?"

"Beautiful."

"What do you do there?"

"It's marvelous. I've never had a better time. I was there for a week; I could have stayed a century. I could have stayed for the rest of my life. It was beautiful."

"What did you do there?"

"Listen, this is a place where they pay attention to detail. Everything is perfect, down to the smallest detail. The little things, like shower curtains and water faucets and silverware and headboards on the beds. Every minor detail is flawless. You'll just adore it."

Clark paused. "Why will I adore it?"

"Because it's perfect. Because you can do anything and everything there. Name it, and there are the most modern, up-to-date—"

"Such as?"

"Anything," Ron Harmon said, "just anything. Listen, this resort is great. It's a whole new departure in travel and entertainment. You'll love it."

"Why?"

Harmon frowned. "Name something?"

"Coprophagia."

"Done!" Harmon said. "The finest, most complete facilities—"

"But coprophagia is eating fec—"

"Doesn't matter! If human beings do it, this resort is set up to permit the most advanced, the most—"

"What?"

"Let me begin at the beginning," Harmon said. "This resort is located in the Caribbean, right? Okay. The first thing is, nobody knows exactly where it is. It's a huge secret. You fly to Miami, and then stop over in Nassau, and from there you take an airplane *with no windows* to this island. Everyone assumes it's one of the Exumas of the Bahamas, but nobody knows for sure. It's a seaplane, and when you land—"

"At San Cristobal?"

"Yes. At San Cristobal, once you land there, you find yourself in the most superb, fully equipped, fantastic resort. You'll adore it. You'll love every minute of it."

"But what do you do there? Tennis? Swimming? Golf? What?"

"*Everything*," Ron Harmon said. "It's just fabulous."

Clark sat down. He stared at Harmon for a long time.

"Confirm my flight to Mexico City," he said.

"You're making a big mistake," Harmon said.

"I want to go to Mexico."

"Mexico is *nothing*."

"I want to go there."

"You're crazy," Harmon said, digging into his desk for the files once more.

9
THE BEST

At eight, Clark met Janice Connor at Orloff's. She wore a black dress scooped as low as the brassiere engineers would allow; her hair was piled high as the hairdresser could manage; she looked very elegant, and rather precarious.

"Smashing," he said.

"Thank you," she said.

Orloff's was not a restaurant Clark frequently visited. For one thing, it was expensive. For another, it was Hollywood. Looking around, he saw several noted stars. Clark disliked Hollywood heartily. He thought it unworldly, foolish, vain, and self-centered. But it was also glamorous, and Janice was drinking in the glamour.

While they waited for a table, Janice told him that she had once been a UCLA cheerleader, and that she had majored in psychology; that was how she had started working for Dr. Shine. He was really an interesting man, with his theories of hypnosis and so forth. Did Clark know that he treated a lot of witches?

No, Clark said, he hadn't known.

"Well, he does," Janice Connor said.

They ordered dinner. The wine came; when it was poured Janice reached into her purse, took out a pill, and gulped it back, swallowing it with wine.

"What was that?"

"Headache pill. I have a headache."

"But what was it?"

"Something new. Phenimol."

"It's addicting."

"Addicting, schmaddicting," Janice Connor said. She smiled at him and leaned forward over the table, her low-cut gown well displayed.

"You're not worried about it?"

"Not at all. If it was dangerous, would my doctor give it to me?"

"I don't know," Clark said.

"He wouldn't," Janice said. She smiled at him. "You're so serious."

"Not really."

The appetizers came. When they finished, Janice reached in her purse for another pill, swallowed it, and gulped wine.

"What was that?"

"I'd rather not say."

"Why not?"

"Well, it's a little embarrassing."

"How do you mean?"

"Well, I was tense, is all. That was two hundred of meprobamate."

"Oh."

"I take it when I'm tense."

"Oh."

"But it doesn't mean anything. I mean, not personally. Frankly, I find you very attractive. Are you on something?"

"Like what?"

"You know. Some kick or other."

"No."

"That's surprising," Janice said. "I mean, I would have thought doctors would have access to all this stuff..."

"We do."

"And you don't take it? Listen, I was once up on dex for a week. It was unbelievable. I'll never forget it."

"How do you mean?"

"Have you ever made love on dex? I don't want to embarrass you. I meant it just as, you know, a question. Have you ever made it on dex? It's great. Fantastic."

"Oh."

"Just great." She reached into her purse and withdrew another pill.

As she swallowed it, she said, "That was the you-know-what."

"Oh."

"Yeah." She dug her elbow into his ribs.

———

Her apartment was small but stylish, with very modern, spare furniture. He looked around. "Nervous? Here, have one of these." She opened a small case on the coffee table, and took out a tiny gray pill. She passed him his drink. "Go ahead. Take it."

"What is it?"

"B twelve. Twenty-five mikes. Really give you a lift."

He shook his head. "No thanks."

"No, go on, take it."

He looked at the pill, very small in his palm. "I don't need it."

"Need it? Of course you don't need it. But it will make you

feel better, all the same. Listen, you ever take ascorbic acid? Really heavy, like twenty-four hundred millis a day? You know how that makes you feel, sort of vibrant all over? Well, this is better."

He protested for a while, but she was insistent, and finally he took it, popping it into his mouth, washing it down with the martini. She had made a very strong martini; it burned all the way down to his stomach, where it made everything very warm and glowing, very hot-pink and burning, a stomach that glowed like a beacon-light, shining through his skin and his undershirt and his shirt . . .

She was staring at him.

"Are you all right?" she asked.

It was hitting him very hard, that martini, going right from his stomach to his head, where his brain was turning a charming pink.

Very, very charming.

"Do you like my nipples?" she asked.

He was staring at her and she was turning out the lights, the room was going dark, very slowly and peacefully dark, and he was feeling tired in a gentle, peaceful sort of way.

"Isn't that lovely?" she asked.

And he said that it was, at least he thought he said so, and then there was an elephant, a large gray elephant tromping through the high grass, where the cheetah waited, sly and muscular, the cheetah in the high grass, waiting, patiently, but the muscles tensed beneath a smooth fur coat, the muscles flexing in an absent, animal way as the elephant came closer, and closer still, moving up heavily to where the cheetah lay slinking in the high green grass.

"Well?" she said.

He heard her, from a great distance.

"What is this?" he said.

She laughed.

Her laugh echoed through the room, and through his ears, huge ears cupping the sound . . .

"What did you give me?" he said.

She laughed again, her voice cracking like ice on the rooftops, melting in the sun, dripping from the shingles onto the snowy ground.

"Isn't it wonderful?" she said.

"What is?"

"It?" She laughed. "Peruvian Green, they call it. It's manufactured in Peru. It affects your mind."

"No kidding," he said. His voice was thick and heavy, as if he were talking submerged in a huge vat of maple syrup. A huge, thick brown vat.

This has happened to me before, he thought.

"It is ineffective," she said, "except with alcohol. You have to drink when you take it. That starts the reaction."

"Reaction?"

"Bubble, bubble," she laughed. "Toil and trouble . . ."

Fires burning around a huge vat, the liquid boiling, the steam rising around shadowy figures. Dancing around the boiling liquid.

"Peruvian Green," she said. "They call it supergrass."

"Do they."

"Yes. They do."

"And what do they call that?" he said, looking at her.

"They call that," she said, "what nasty little girls do to nasty little boys."

He felt that was rather interesting, really quite worthy of

further and deeper consideration, and he was about to think about it, think quite carefully and coolly about it, when he found he wasn't thinking anymore.

The world began to race for him, to pick up speed and momentum, until it was rushing like a train out of control, an airplane crashing to earth, whining and whistling in the wind, with the ground rushing up.

And then his head exploded, and he saw white pure light for several blinding instants.

And then nothing.

PART II
EDEN

> *"If an urn lacks the characteristics of an urn, how can we call it an urn?"*
> **SAYING OF CONFUCIUS**

10
A FEELING OF POWER

He opened his eyes. It was dark. Through the open window, he could see the moon, hazy through the smog. He coughed and looked around him. He was lying on a couch, alone in the room. He sat up slowly. Someone had put a blanket over him; it fell away and he felt the cool night air.

He stood, expecting to feel shaky. But he was calm; in fact, he felt good. He had a sensation of being fully awake, alert, and calm.

A very peculiar feeling: there was a kind of intensity to it that was almost disturbing. He looked around the room once more. It was unfamiliar in the night, a strange and bizarre room.

He caught himself.

He was back in his own apartment.

"That's funny," he said.

His own apartment. He went from the living room to the bedroom, still not quite believing. The bedroom was empty, the bed neatly made. Which could only mean . . .

He looked down at the coffee table in the living room. The newspaper was there: Tuesday, October 10.

But he had taken Janice to dinner on the eighth. The night of the eighth. And that meant—

He rubbed his eyes. Two days? Was it possible? Had he really been here two days?

He wandered around the apartment, unable to understand. In the kitchen, there was an empty coffee cup, with a cigarette stubbed out in the saucer. There were traces of lipstick on the cigarette.

Beside the saucer was a photograph, torn out from the newspaper. It showed Sharon Wilder sitting on a suitcase, miniskirt high to show long smooth legs. She was smiling, sitting very straight, breasts thrown forward to the photographers. The caption read: "Sharon Wilder To Resort." Resort to what? he wondered, squinting to read the fine print in the darkness. It said that Sharon Wilder, Hollywood starlet, was leaving for the new resort of San Cristobal.

By the front door he found the rest of his mail, unopened. Included in the stack was a telegram, which he tore open. It was from the Aero Travel Agency:

```
WHERE ARE YOU? AIRLINES AND HOTEL
CANCELED RESERVATIONS BECAUSE OF FAILURE
TO PAY DEPOSIT.
CALL IMMEDIATELY.
                              RON
```

"Hell," he said, staring at the telegram. That was annoying. What was he going to do now?

Drive. Perhaps he would drive south. It would be good, to make the trip by car . . .

The telephone rang. He looked at his watch, wondering at the time, but his watch was stopped.

"Hell."

He picked up the phone.

"Dr. Clark."

"Roger?" A female voice. "This is Sharon."

"Sharon? I thought you were gone."

"No, silly. I was about to leave, but the flight was canceled. Mechanical difficulties. I won't leave until tomorrow morning."

"Oh. What time is it?"

"One fifteen. Did I wake you?"

"No."

"Good. Are you all right, Roger?"

"Yes."

"You sound a little groggy."

"I'm fine," he said. He didn't feel groggy. He didn't feel the least bit groggy. He felt clear-headed and fine, very fine.

"Roger?"

"Yes."

"There was something I wanted to ask you."

"Yes?"

"About the trip."

She paused. He waited. "I'm alone," she said. "As it turns out."

"Oh."

"And I have two tickets. They were given to me."

"Oh."

"And it seems a shame to waste one."

"Yes, it does."

There was a moment of silence. "Roger, are you all right?"

"What time?" he said.

"Nine-fifteen."

"All right," he said.

"Check in an hour before flight."

"An hour before."

"And pack light clothes."

"Fine," he said.

"You're a love," she said. "Good night." He heard a smacking sound as she kissed the phone, and he hung up, feeling a strange sense of power.

11
OLIVE OR TWIST?

He had to knock on the door for several minutes before anyone answered. And then it was Jerry, pulling the bathrobe around his waist, looking tired and cross.

"Jerry, I have to talk to you."

Jerry Barnes blinked in the light of the hallway. "Rog? Is that you?"

"Yes," Clark said. "Listen, I have to talk to you, it's important."

"Rog . . ." Jerry fumbled with the robe, pulling back one sleeve to look at his watch. "It's three o'clock in the morning."

"I know," Clark said, walking into the apartment. "I'll barely have time to pack."

"Pack?" Jerry was scratching his head, looking at him. "Pack what?"

Clark went into the living room, sat down, and turned on a light. Jerry winced.

"Jerry," he said, "you're a stockbroker, and I need—"

"I'm a stockbroker," Jerry said, "from nine to five. Less, if I can help it. At three in the morning I'm—"

"Jerry," called a sleepy voice from the bedroom. "Is something wrong?"

"No, love," Jerry said, frowning at Clark. He moved close and whispered: "Can't we make it another time, Rog? Huh?"

"Who is it?" Clark said.

"Linda. A little dividend." Jerry managed a sleepy grin. "She just split three for two."

"That sounds exciting."

"Tiring," Jerry said, rubbing his face. "Very tiring."

"You selling long or short these days, Jerry?"

"Rog," he said, "for Pete's sake, it's three in the morning—"

"I need information. About a corporation."

"Jer-ry," called the sleepy voice. "Come back home to momma."

Jerry rolled his eyes and looked at Clark. "This really is a bad time, Rog, no kidding."

Clark got up and went to the refrigerator. Jerry Barnes always had a pitcher of martinis in the refrigerator. He poured himself one, looked inquiringly at Jerry, who nodded; he poured a second one.

"Make it quick, huh?"

"Okay, Jerry. Very quick. I want to know about a corporation in Santa Monica called Advance."

Jerry Barnes gulped his drink and said, "Oh no. Not another one. You too? How about an olive?"

"Twist," Clark said, swirling the cold liquid in the glass.

Jerry dropped a twist of lemon into it. "Everybody wants to know about Advance."

"Everybody?"

"At least six people have called me in the last month. They've seen the building, or heard about the corporation, and they're interested. I checked it out a while ago."

"And?"

He shook his head. "Not for sale. Private corp. It's not on the big board, it's not on the American, it's not anywhere. The stock is all privately held."

"What else do you know?"

Jerry Barnes took a long gulp of the drink, and rubbed his face again. He seemed to be waking up. "It's a funny bunch, Advance. Started two years ago with a handful of wizard-types, doing biological research. They were located in Florida then. The original group, which includes the president, this guy Harvey Blood, was all marine scientists."

"No kidding."

"And they were doing government research. They discovered a thing called SVD."

"Which is?"

"A viral disease of sharks, transmitted in the, uh, sexual secretions or whatever it is that sharks do."

"SVD?"

"Stands for shark venereal disease. Locally known as the finny clap."

"Jerry, are you pulling my leg?"

"At three in the morning? Come on."

"Jer-ry, ba-by . . ."

"In a minute, love," Jerry said, pouring himself another martini. "Jeez, Rog, she really is something," he said. "You wouldn't believe it. I used to hear stories about girls like this—"

"Advance," Clark reminded him.

"Yeah, Advance. Anyway, they discovered this fish disease and isolated the virus, or some damned thing, and sold it to the government for a big fee. It was going to be a huge new breakthrough in biological warfare. From there, they went on to investigate Arizona Sleeping Sickness."

"*Arizona—*"

"Shhhhh. Yeah. Arizona Sleeping Sickness. Another new disease they invented. Carried by the eight-legged nymph of the sagebrush caterpillar in northwest Ariz—"

"I hope," said a voice, "that I'm not breaking up the party."

Clark turned. There was a girl standing in the doorway to the bedroom, wearing a man's pajama top and a sleepy frown.

"Linda, this is Roger." Jerry sighed. "Roger is a crazy doctor."

"Oh," Linda said. She padded across the room to the refrigerator and poured herself a drink. "He must be crazy," she said.

"He's also leaving," Jerry said, with a stern look at Clark, who was staring at the girl's legs. They were very nice legs.

"Yes, just leaving," Clark said. "But about Advance—"

"All right, look: the thing about Advance is that they got started with these two diseases, sold them to the government for a big fee, and then moved into the private sector. Completely. They're doing other things now."

"Like what?"

Jerry shrugged. "Nobody seems to know, really. There are rumors about thought control, and drugs, and test-tube engineering... wild stuff. But nobody knows for sure." He sighed. "And anyway, it's not for sale. Okay?"

"Okay," Clark said. He finished his martini and stood.

"Good night, crazy doctor," Linda said, with a sleepy smile. "Nice having you."

"You haven't had him yet," Jerry said.

"Yes," Linda said, "but you never can tell."

12
TRIPPYTIME

"One more! Hold it!"

The flashbulbs popped.

"Now around, that's it. A little leg, Miss Wilder!"

Flashbulbs, white silent explosions in the air. The photographers scurrying, moving around her.

"Give us a smile, Sharon! Good! Another!"

She turned, waved, and smiled once more, then walked up the steps to the airplane. "That's it, boys."

"Aw, Sharon."

"Just one, Sharon."

"Miss Wilder . . ."

But she was climbing the steps, and a moment later ducked through into the interior of the airplane, and moved down the aisle to her seat in the first-class section.

Roger Clark was waiting. He had watched it all from the window seat.

"God, photographers," Sharon said, dropping into her seat. "I hate posing," she said, "in all these clothes. Is the suit all right?"

She wore a severely cut suit of black leather, with a red scarf at her throat.

"The suit is fine," Clark said.

"You're such a dear," Sharon said, and kissed his cheek. She settled back in the seat and buckled her belt. "Well," she said. "At last: it's trippytime, darling."

"So it appears."

"It was good of you to come," she said, "on short notice. I felt terrible about calling you."

"I'm glad you did."

There was a whine as the jet engines were started. The few remaining passengers filed down the aisle to their seats; up in front, they could see the stewardess closing the door. The steps were wheeled away.

"This is going to be a marvelous flight," Sharon said. "I've decided."

Clark said, "What exactly do we do?"

"It's very simple," she said. "We fly direct to Miami. Then we have a little stopover, and get the plane to Nassau. From there, we go by seaplane to San Cristobal."

"Which is where?"

She laughed. "Silly, that's part of the thing. Nobody knows. It's a secret."

Clark remembered seeing the tickets in her bedroom. They had been paid for by Advance. "Tell me," he said. "How did you hear about this place?"

She sighed. "You doctors. You never get away from your patients long enough to . . ."

She picked up the latest issue of *Holiday* magazine and thumbed through it quickly, finally turning back a page. She handed the magazine to Clark.

The full-page ad read:

DRUG OF CHOICE

EDEN ISLAND
Everything Under The Sun

Never was there a resort like this before! Name your game: tennis, swimming, badminton, skin-diving, deep-sea fishing, hunting (wild boar), water-skiing—Eden Island has the finest, most modern facilities for everything. Or you may prefer to spend your time in our casino, dancing and dining at one of our twelve different clubs. Everything has been provided for you, all under the most expert management.

The sun, of course, takes care of itself.

Eden Island: there's never been anything quite like it before.

There was also a large color photograph showing a beach, a dock with sailboats, and back from the shore, secluded in manicured grounds and shaded by palms, an enormous white resort complex of hotels, swimming pools, and tennis courts. It was breathtakingly beautiful.

"Ads like this," Sharon said, "have been running for weeks. Everybody's talking about it. Everybody's going. They say it will be the resort of the century, when it's finished."

"It's not finished?"

"No. San Cristobal—that's the real name of the island—is five square miles. The company that is developing it says they won't finish for twenty years."

"What company is that?"

She shrugged. "Some American corporation."

He looked at her steadily. "Advance?"

"Advance what?"

"The Advance Corporation," Clark said.

For a moment, she seemed puzzled, and then she laughed. "You really did check up on me, didn't you? That's George's company. He's such a dear—but no, Advance has nothing to do with this."

"How do you know?"

"Because George told me about it. They're into all sorts of stuff—electronic control of the brain, and new birth control chemicals—but not *resorts*, love."

"You sure?"

"Of course I'm sure." She was looking at him in an odd way, as if she might become angry.

"Where'd you get the tickets?" he asked.

She shook her head. "You're a glutton for punishment."

"Just curious."

"George got them for me," she said. "You see, I was originally going with him."

"Oh."

"But he canceled out at the last minute. Some conference on enzymes in Detroit." She looked out the window as the plane taxied down the runway, gathered speed, and began to climb into the air.

"And now," she said, "I'd like to change the subject."

An hour later, over drinks, he said, "You were right about one thing. I did check up on you. I even went to see Abraham Shine."

"He's a dear man," Sharon said, biting into a shrimp hors d'oeuvre.

"He mentioned that you were concerned about corporations."

"Concerned? That wasn't it at all." She munched on the shrimp. "I was terrified."

"Why?"

"I don't know. It was this kind of irrational thing, a fear. Like there were so many huge complex companies, and I was just a little person, all alone. I felt . . . powerless."

"And you were worried about—"

"Being controlled," she said, nodding. "I was. It was an awful period in my life. I would go to bed at night and dream that some giant corporation was manipulating me, like a puppet and its master, behind the scenes, pulling the strings. I felt I couldn't control anything, that I was just being tugged this way and that."

"Why did you feel that?"

"Listen," she said, taking a sip of her drink. Her face was already flushed from a previous drink; she looked young and pretty and very sexy. "I'll tell you something. The life of a young girl in this town—I mean LA—is pretty miserable. You want to get into the business, and you grow up thinking, dreaming about it, how wonderful it would be, attending your opening night and climbing out of the limousine wearing a chiffon gown and a white fur coat . . . And then you start working on it, you quit school one day at sixteen and you say the hell with algebra, I'm going to make pictures, and you start working. You get an agent. I had a jerk named Morrie Sandwell. He set up some meetings with producers, sort of introducing me around. The producers explained how tough it was for a newcomer to break in, how a new girl really needed the guiding touch of an experienced person in the business, someone with contacts. So okay, you get your contacts, you go along with the touch, because you have that dream of the opening night, and getting out of the limousine and looking up at the marquee with your name there. It's a good dream."

She pushed her drink away.

"And then one day you wake up and realize what the hell you've been doing, hanging around with a bunch of nasty old guys and nasty old hotel rooms and too many drinks and too many sour laughs. And all you've got to show for it is a walk-on in *Gunslinger* and two lines as the cook in *Gorman's Heroes*. And you just see it, clear and plain: you've been used."

"And then?"

"Then you start seeing someone like Dr. Shine. He was very good for me. He got me out of this corporation manipulation thing, and into something else. He made me believe that I could control my destiny. So I fired my agent, got a new one, and started fresh. I played with a new set of rules—my rules—and it was a whole new game."

She looked at him steadily.

"And I'm winning," she said. "This time, I'm winning."

―――

It was raining in Miami—a cold, October rain that presaged a hurricane brewing to the south. They had two hours in the airport and wandered around together, looking at the shops, having a hamburger and a drink. Then Sharon said she wanted to try on sweaters in one of the airport stores, and Clark went off by himself. He walked aimlessly, not paying much attention to anything.

And then he realized.

He was being followed. It was a short man with a plastic clear raincoat which showed a rumpled blue suit underneath. Clark walked on, then looked back.

The man was still there. He had a bland, expressionless face. Clark wondered if he was one of the passengers on the plane, but could not recall his face. But he was attentive when he boarded flight 409 from Miami to Nassau, New Providence.

The man in the raincoat did not board the plane with him. Odd, he thought. Sharon was already in her seat. As he sat down, he said, "Find anything?"

"No," she said, "they were all wrong for me."

There was a hazy, humid sun in Nassau. They were met at the small terminal by a representative of Eden Island, who helped them all through Bahamian customs with remarkable ease, and then led them outside to a bus. It was a normal sort of bus, except that it was painted flame red and hot orange, with black lettering on the side: EDEN ISLAND EXPRESS.

They climbed aboard and were given grapes and other fruit while the man explained that the bus would take them to the seaplane.

"Purely a temporary arrangement, folks," the man said. "You see, we haven't yet built the airstrip on Eden. But they're working on it. Of course," he said, "most people find a seaplane quite an experience, yes indeed, quite an experience."

Clark stared out the window for the duration of the dreary trip from the airport to the port of Nassau, set down beneath the crest upon which the old fort was erected. The bus drove directly to the waterfront, and pulled up before a large seaplane. Everyone got on board.

The passenger section was quite dark; the windows had all been covered with black paint.

"So it's true," Clark said.

"Oh yes," Sharon said. "The location is a big secret." She smiled. "Of course, it's only a publicity stunt. By now all sorts of people in private planes and yachts will have found the island and charted it. But it's a good gimmick."

Drinks were brought around as soon as the plane was in the air, but Clark didn't have one. He was tired, and the monotony of the dark cabin was conducive to sleep. He must have dozed off, because when he awoke the airplane was rocking in a steady, rhythmic way, and he could not hear the sound of the propellers.

"What's happened?"

"We landed," Sharon said, smiling. "They just tied up to the dock."

The passengers were already beginning to stand and stretch in the aisles.

Clark said, "But if we're tied up, then—"

"In a few moments, we'll see Eden Island," Sharon said, and smiled with radiant excitement.

The forward door was opened, and sunlight streamed into the cabin. The passengers began to file outside.

13
EAST OF SAN CRISTOBAL

His first sensation was of the air: it was clear and warm and redolent of foreign scents, strange spices. Though the sun was setting behind the far hills of the island, and the sky beginning to deepen to purple, the air remained warm, with a mild breeze. He breathed deeply and looked around him.

The dock was thronged with porters and passengers and baggage, but looking up from the dock he could see a smooth white beach, with the water lapping gently against the land. Farther back was a structure which appeared to be the hotel. He could not see the tennis courts and swimming pools which he had seen in the photograph in the ad, and he assumed they were farther back inland.

Though newly constructed, the hotel had a quaint appearance; it had been built in a rather Spanish manner, with graceful arches leading into small gardens and terraces. There were flowers everywhere, lending smell as well as color to the scene. Sharon clapped her hands. "Isn't it beautiful?" Clark had to agree that it was, but as he looked around, it seemed to him that something was wrong. He could not define it for several minutes, but then, as he walked up the dock with Sharon, it struck him.

"Kind of deserted," he said. "Nobody on the beach. Nobody much around the hotel. It's almost as if—"

"Probably," Sharon said, "everybody is inside changing for dinner. A day in this sun can be exhausting, you know."

"But the beach is smooth. There isn't a footprint or—"

"Silly. They brush it down."

"They what?"

"Every night. They brush it down. Men come along with big brushes and sort of comb it. Like a horse."

"Oh."

As he came up to the hotel, he decided that his impression was incorrect. While registering at the desk, he could faintly hear the *thwock!* of tennis balls, a game being played on some distant court; and he could hear splashing and laughter from a pool.

At the desk, he left Sharon, following his own porter to his room. It was a pleasant single room overlooking the beach and the dock; directly beneath his balcony was a courtyard with a bar and a polished wooden floor. Undoubtedly it was used for dancing in the evening.

The room was comfortably furnished with a bed, a desk, and a television . . .

He paused. A television?

This island must be hundreds of miles from the nearest television station. They could not possibly hope to receive—

Abruptly, the screen glowed to life. It was a color set; he found himself staring at a pleasant, white-haired man in formal attire.

"Good evening, Dr. Clark," the man said. "I am your manager, Mr. Lefevre. Allow me to take this opportunity to welcome you personally to Eden Island. I hope that in the next few days we can make your stay with us truly memorable. If there is anything which is not to your utmost satisfaction, please do not hesitate to report it to me. The television, by the way, is closed-circuit; feature films are shown twice a day at seven and ten. The waiter will be arriving at your room shortly with a drink and a bowl of fruit. Please accept it with our compliments, and our best wishes for a pleasant stay here."

The screen went blank.

"I'll be damned," he said, and there was a knock at the door. A boy in a red jacket with gold buttons came in with a drink on a silver tray in one hand, and a bowl of fruit in the other.

"Compliments of the management, Dr. Clark," he said. "If you need anything further, please call us."

Clark reached into his pocket for a tip.

"No, sir, thank you anyway," the boy said, and closed the door as he left.

Clark looked at the fruit basket, and then at the drink. It was a rather peculiar drink, foamy and orange with cherries in the bottom. There was a small card alongside it, on the tray.

"Mango punch is a specialty of the island. It has been a native favorite for centuries. Enjoy it with our compliments."

He sipped it cautiously: it was tangy, bittersweet, and very strong. He took a second sip, and decided he liked it.

He took the drink onto the balcony and sat down in a comfortable deck chair, and propped his legs up on the railing. From here, he could look down over the bar and the dance floor, and out to the dock, where the sailboats rocked gently in the soft wind as night fell. It was peaceful and quiet, though he could still hear the distant sound of a tennis game, and an occasional whoop of laughter from the pool.

It was, he decided, going to be an extremely pleasant vacation.

The telephone rang, and he was about to go inside to answer it when he saw there was an extension on the balcony.

"They think of everything," he said, and picked it up.

"Hello?"

"Roger? Sharon. Listen, isn't it beautiful? Isn't it the most wonderful place you've ever been? Have you tasted the mango punch?"

He agreed that it was all very wonderful, and they arranged to meet in an hour for drinks before dinner. He went back inside to unpack and take a shower. While he was unpacking, he heard an odd humming sound. At first he could not locate the source of the noise; it was very soft, almost a droning. He walked around the room, listening.

And then he realized it was coming from the television set. Funny, he thought. He made a mental note to tell the management about it. He slapped the set once, with the flat of his hand. The sound stopped.

"Well," he said, "that's that." Life for Roger Clark became a kind of idyll. After the first day, he stopped wearing his watch, and when, after three days, he chanced to pick it up, he saw that it had stopped. He didn't care. It seemed almost fitting, that time should stop on this island. He was having a superb time.

The first night, he had had dinner with Sharon in the hotel, and had been pleasantly surprised at the excellence of the food. Afterward, they had gone to a discotheque, one of three on the new resort island. It had been a smashing, vibrant place; he had gotten drunk and enjoyed himself thoroughly.

The next day he had played tennis with Sharon, and discovered that she was a blood player, a true fighter. She wore a very short white skirt and a very tight white blouse, and used her wiles to distract him whenever she could; he was beaten miserably in the first set. On the next two sets he fought back, winning the third 22–20. Then, exhausted, hot, and laughing, they had swum in the Olympic pool, before lying in the sun to dry. They had dinner at a native restaurant where they were served squid and other strange things, but it was all excellent. They made passionate love and he slept soundly afterward.

The next day was more of the same; the day after, they took a sailboat out and sailed around the north tip of the island, passing a coastline of rugged beauty. They went skin-diving in a warm sea alive with fish, brightly colored, darting about.

He felt marvelous.

The next day, he played tennis so vigorously that he broke his stringing; Sharon laughed, he bought her a drink, and they went back to his room in the middle of the afternoon.

And so it went, day after day. Every once in a while, one of the other guests—and the guests were an unusually congenial and interesting group of people, it seemed to Clark—would come up and say, "Isn't this fantastic? Isn't this ideal?"

And Clark would have to agree. It was absolutely, completely, totally ideal.

He awoke in the middle of the night with a strange kind of abruptness; one moment he was asleep, the next moment he was wide awake, staring at the ceiling of his room.

Something was wrong.

He knew it with frightening certainty. Something was wrong. He could not say what it was, but he was quite sure.

He lay in his bed and listened.

He heard the sound of the ocean, carried on the wind through the open doors to the balcony. He heard the chattering of some nocturnal bird, hidden in the trees around the hotel.

Otherwise, nothing.

He sat up. The room was familiar, his room, his bed, his desk in the corner, with the letter to Ron Harmon at Aero that he had begun to write, but had never managed to finish. Propped up against one wall was his tennis racket with the broken string.

It was all perfectly normal. He sat up slowly, trying to decide what disturbed him. He got out of bed and walked toward the bathroom, and as he did so, he kicked something on the floor.

He turned on the light and looked.

A tray.

It was a simple iron tray, scratched and battered, the tray of a cheap all-night cafeteria. There was a bowl of soup on the tray, thin yellow gruel, now cold. Next to the bowl was a plate of unappetizing hash, and a glass of water.

He stared at the tray for a long time. It seemed absurd, this cheap tray and this awful food, sitting in his room. How had it gotten there?

He looked closely. The hash had been partially eaten; a fork lay on the plate. He scooped up a bite of the hash and tasted it.

Awful. Revolting. He went to the bathroom to spit it out, turning on the light, and—

He stared at his image in the mirror. His eyes were pink and haggard; he had a heavy growth of beard, at least several days' worth; his skin was pale.

And then, as he stood in the bathroom, he heard the growl of thunder, and the wind blew more strongly. He frowned, spit out the hash, and walked onto the balcony.

He could hardly believe his eyes.

The dock was bare; the boats had all been taken in and lashed to the trees on shore. The beach was wet and ugly-looking. Beneath him, the polished wood dance floor was soaked, puddles standing about everywhere; the bar was closed down, and covered with a canvas tarpaulin. He looked at the flowers on the balcony, which had climbed snaking through the railing. They were closed, beaten down by rain, battered-looking.

As he stood there, the first drops of rain began to fall from leaden skies, and the thunder rolled again.

My God, he thought. It's been raining here for days.

How long had it been?

He went back to the bathroom and urinated, shivering with a new and chilling fear. It was so terrifying, he was not really surprised when he looked down and saw that his urine was a bright, fluorescent blue.

14
GAINFUL EMPLOYMENT

He dressed quickly, slipping into a pair of slacks, sneakers, and a sweater. He had brought only one sweater, and now he was glad; it was cold.

When he had dressed, he looked again at the tray and the gruel set out by his bed.

Then he left the room. The hallway was quiet, he moved slowly down toward the stairs at the far end, avoiding the elevator. Around him, the hotel was silent except for the rising sound of the storm.

He reached the head of the stairs and paused. On the ground floor below, he could hear quiet voices, and shuffling sounds. As he waited, he heard footsteps approaching, and then coming up the stairs.

He had a moment of panic, backing away. Then he saw a closet marked "Utility"; the door was not locked, and he slipped in among mops and buckets. He left the door slightly ajar and waited.

After several moments, two people appeared at the top of the stairs. One was a lovely young woman in a bikini; the other was a red-jacketed waiter. They walked slowly, arm in arm, down the hallway. The girl seemed a little unsteady, and often leaned against her companion for support. Once or twice, she giggled.

Eventually, they came to her room, and stopped. The waiter unlocked the girl's door, choosing the key from a large ring at his belt. The girl put her arms around his neck and kissed him soundly.

"Thank you for a lovely evening, darling," she said. And then, "Shall we . . ."

"By all means," the waiter said. He held the door open, and the girl went into her room.

"You make such thrilling love," the girl said.

"Yes, my dear," the waiter said, and closed the door. After a few moments, he reappeared in the hallway, walked down two doors, and unlocked another door. He disappeared inside, and came out with a stocky middle-aged man at his side.

"Ah," said the man. "Charming morning, eh, Linda?"

"Oh yes," the waiter said.

"All this sunlight . . . makes a man feel marvelous!"

"It certainly does," the waiter said.

"After breakfast, we'll play a little tennis, shall we?"

"That would be nice," the waiter said.

"Good girl, Linda," the man said.

They passed Clark, and headed down the stairs. He waited until he could no longer hear their footsteps, then came out of the closet.

Slowly, he made his way downstairs.

When he reached the bottom, he could peer around the corner and look at the lobby. He remembered it as a charming place with a simple desk and polished marble floors; lots of flowers everywhere. But now it was completely transformed. A broad, thick plastic mat of silver foil had been set out on the floor. It was very large, perhaps twenty yards square, and on it a dozen guests sprawled in bathing suits. Overhead was a bank of sunlamps, blazing down on the mat and the guests.

Five or six waiters were in attendance. At intervals an alarm would buzz softly, and the waiter would go up to the guests, and gently help them to turn over. The guests followed instructions with happy, complacent smiles on their faces. They all seemed quite awake, and would exchange a few words with the waiters at each turning.

Among themselves, the waiters spoke in low, disgruntled tones.

"Pain in the ass," one said.

"It'll blow over soon, then we can work it as usual. An hour on the balcony each day."

"I hate this. Whenever there's a storm, this damned schedule."

Another waiter laughed. "Can't have our guests going home without a tan, can we?"

"Oh no, that would never do."

Clark waited several minutes until he understood what was happening. Then he slipped around the corner, moving from the stair toward the registration desk. No one saw him. The waiters were not attentive—and why should they be? Every guest here was drugged to the ears.

At the desk he paused, ducking down into shadow. To his left was the terrace, and beyond that the swimming pool and the tennis courts. He moved off, outside, into the rainy darkness.

His sneakers squished softly on the dance floor. It was then that he noticed, with surprise, that it was not really wood but a kind of plastic. Very realistic plastic.

From the dance floor, he headed off into the gardens. Down a narrow, damp path to the swimming pool, which was located—

He stopped.

There was no swimming pool. None at all. There was a high diving board; he had seen that when he had first arrived, sticking up over the trees. But the diving board was sunk in concrete, surrounded by dirt.

No pool.

He frowned. He remembered it so clearly: a beautiful sparkling Olympic pool, with a high board at one end, and a bar at the other end where you could stand waist-deep in water and drink mango punches until you were sleepy; then you could crawl out and lie on one of the deck chairs, located on the broad concrete deck around the pool.

What the hell?

He padded across the dirt beneath the board; it was now rather muddy with rain. He went on, toward the tennis courts, all twelve of them, beautifully maintained, the white lines carefully laid out each day.

Once again, he paused.

No tennis courts.

Instead there was only a small metal shack, standing in the midst of scrubby vegetation. He opened the door to the shack and found some electronic equipment, including a tape recorder.

He flicked it on.

Thwock!... Thwock!

A woman's laugh, and a man's deeper chuckle.

Thwock!

He flicked it off. The sounds died.

"Very neat," he said aloud.

"We think so," a voice replied. He turned and saw the smiling, white-haired man whom he recognized as Mr. Lefevre, the manager.

"I see you're ready for work," Lefevre said.

"Work?"

"Yes, of course. Come this way, please." He looked up at the sky. "Ugly night. It'll pour, any minute. We'd best get inside, don't you think?"

Dazed, he followed Lefevre back through the underbrush to the hotel. They walked into the lobby where the waiters were still turning the guests beneath the sunlamps; the waiters nodded politely to Clark. They did not seem surprised to see him.

"This way, Dr. Clark," Lefevre said. He led him into a private office, comfortably furnished, and closed the door.

"You're soaked through," Lefevre said. "There's a towel in the bathroom"—he nodded to a door—"that you might want to use. Wouldn't do to catch a cold, you know. Matter of fact, that's one of the problems you're going to face very shortly."

"What's that?"

"Colds, Dr. Clark. We try to guard against them, but . . ." He shrugged.

Clark went into the bathroom, took a towel, and rubbed his hair. "Listen," he said, "I don't know what's going on here, but there's some kind of mistake—"

"No mistake," Lefevre said, smiling.

"But I don't understand. You people are—"

"On the contrary, Dr. Clark. You understand perfectly. We people are operating a resort which does not exist. As you demonstrated to your own satisfaction just a few moments ago. We have a facade—this building, the rooms upstairs—but behind that, there is nothing. Everything else that is needed, we supply by means of the drug."

Clark nodded. "The drug that turns urine blue."

"Precisely. A most useful drug. You see, doctor, we are

engaged in a kind of experiment here, an experiment in perception. We know, indeed everybody knows, that perception is altered by mental state. You may dine in the finest restaurant in the world, and eat the most superb food, but if you are in a bad mood, if your business has just gone bankrupt, if your wife has just left you, then this delicious, excellent food will taste like sawdust. And conversely: a ghastly meal in a tawdry restaurant may seem like a king's banquet if your mental state is disposed to make it so."

"I don't see what all this—"

"All this," Lefevre said, waving his hand around, "all this is a kind of extreme experiment. We assume that mental state colors our experience irrespective of objective reality. Normally, one must control experience in an attempt to produce the correct mental state—to be happy, healthy, and carefree, one must spend vast sums to go to some resort where your whims are realized. But suppose that the mental state could be controlled independent of experience? Eh? What then?"

"The drug," Clark said.

"Yes indeed. It is the drug of choice for controlling mental state. It produces mental . . . well, *pliability*. Suggestiveness is heightened to an extraordinary degree. One is receptive to suggestion, any suggestion, and one will live quite happily within the framework of that suggestion until another suggestion is supplied."

"My tennis racket."

"Exactly. Two days ago, one of the boys went into your room, cut a string on your racket, and suggested to you that you had broken it in a fierce game of tennis. You accepted that idea quite happily."

"I've been on the drug all that time?"

"Oh yes. From your first mango punch. And, of course, the sound . . ."

"In the television?"

"Yes. It is a particular frequency, which can be duplicated with a tuning fork, such as this one here." He held up a small, polished fork, and struck it against the table. It hummed softly.

"This fork vibrates at 423 cycles. That is a resonant frequency of an audio output of the brain's alpha waves. A normal person finds it no more than a passing irritant. But under the influence of the drug—well, shall I show you?"

Clark said, "Please do."

"Very well."

They went outside; Lefevre said to the waiters, "Anyone making love tonight?"

One waiter said, "The one in room 24."

"Has she been sounded yet?"

"No. Not yet."

"All right."

He led Clark to the elevator; they rode up to the second floor, and went down the corridor to room 24. Lefevre unlocked it and went in.

A girl lay on the bed. It was the same girl that Clark had seen earlier, walking upstairs with the waiter. She was a pretty young blond with a white bikini.

She sat up and smiled uncertainly as they entered. "Darling?" she said, in a questioning voice.

"Yes, darling," Lefevre said. "It's me."

"Oh," the girl said, smiling happily, "I was waiting for you."

"I'm here now."

She smiled, then looked at Clark. "But have you brought someone else with you?"

"No, darling. You must be mistaken. I am alone."

"Oh," the girl said, staring right at Clark. "I must have been mistaken. Do you love me very much?"

"Very much, darling."

"Have you come to make love to me?"

"Yes," Lefevre said.

"I'm glad," the girl said.

"You just undress, and get into bed," Lefevre said. "I'm going into the bathroom for a moment."

"All right," the girl said. She stood up and began to remove her bikini. Clark and Lefevre remained standing near the bed.

"I don't think you can hear me talking in the bathroom, darling," Lefevre said.

"No, I can't," she said.

"You see," Lefevre said to Clark, "she is totally happy with sensations which she manufactures for herself. You'll notice the tentative way she speaks. That is because she requires the baseline stimulus, the minimal directions, from someone on the outside. From me. Whatever I tell her, she accepts. If I tell her you are not in the room, then of course you are not."

Clark said, "Who does she think you are?"

"I don't know," Lefevre said. "And I don't want to push it. You'll soon come to understand that people on this drug have a way of telling you what kind of sensations they want to experience. She undoubtedly thinks I'm her husband or lover or whoever it is she wants to believe I am. I have done nothing to change that preconception. If I were to announce, for example, that I were her father, then she would panic. But I haven't announced that. I have only followed her cues, and reinforced the appropriate ones."

"And she accepts this, because of the drug."

"Yes. But the drug has other powers, a whole new order of powers on a scale quite undreamed of. Because when she hears the sound of the tuning fork—well, watch for yourself."

The girl was by now in bed, the sheets pulled up to her chin. She stared calmly at the ceiling.

"Darling," she said.

"I'm here," Lefevre said. "I love you."

The girl did not move. She continued to stare at the ceiling.

"You make love beautifully," she said.

Abruptly, Lefevre struck the tuning fork. The girl's eyes snapped shut and her body went rigid for a moment and then relaxed. She seemed suddenly fast asleep.

Clark began to understand. "She's in a coma," he said.

"Yes. Unarousable for a period of twelve to sixteen hours, but quite safe, I assure you. In fact she is experiencing sensations of fantastic pleasure. That is the beauty of the drug: it stimulates hypothalamic pleasure centers directly, in combination with the correct auditory stimuli. For twelve hours she will experience nothing but pure, total, delightful pleasure."

"And afterward?"

"She will get more drugs. And more again, up until the morning of her departure. The doses will be tapered on that final day; she will be just beginning to awake fully when she is aboard the seaplane, taking off for Nassau. When she wakes up, she will be refreshed, tanned, invigorated—and she will carry beautiful memories back with her."

"All quite neat."

"Yes indeed," Lefevre said. "This drug is a significant breakthrough."

They walked out of the room, down the hallway. Clark said, "What exactly is the drug?"

"We're not certain. It hasn't been fully analyzed yet."

"But you're administering it—"

"Oh yes," Lefevre said, with a wave of his hand, "but it's quite safe. You can see that for yourself. Perfectly safe."

"What's it called?"

"It hasn't got a name. After all, why name it? Who needs

to know its name? It will never be marketed, never be made available to the public. Can you imagine what would happen if it were available?" Lefevre shook his head. "The whole world would be lying around in a coma. Industry would grind to a halt. Commerce would cease. Wars would end in mid-battle. Life as we know it would simply *stop*."

Clark said nothing.

"When we at Advance developed this drug, we were aware of its potential. We were most careful to guard it, and to plan for its limited commercial use. In this setting, you see, the drug is superb. People come here, have a fine time, and go home refreshed and happy. They return to normal, active lives none the worse for their experience—indeed, much improved. Don't you think we've accomplished something marvelous?"

"No," Clark said.

"That's very odd," Lefevre said. "An opinion like that, coming from an employee of the corporation."

"What corporation?"

"Advance, of course. Why do you think we woke you up? You've got to start working right now."

Back in his office, Lefevre showed him the material. "You see," he said, "there's no question about it. You are an employee of Advance. Here is the contract you signed when you visited the Santa Monica office."

He pushed a photostat of a form across the desk.

"*I* signed—"

And then he remembered the little lady at the desk. There was something that he had signed.

"And your picture, of course. Shaking hands with Harvey Blood, president of the Corporation. Shaking hands with George K. Washington. The contract states, by the way, that you have full knowledge of the experimental drug, and have agreed to supervise activities at the resort for the month."

He smiled.

"And here," he said, "is a canceled check, deposited to your account. And another check, here. And a third. Totaling slightly more than seven thousand dollars. So you see, you're an employee, all right. And a rather well-paid employee at that."

Clark said nothing. He was thinking over everything, from the beginning, from the Angel, and then Sharon . . .

"This was all planned," he said. "You planned a way to get me out here, you engineered it all—"

"Let's say," Lefevre said, "that we helped you to make up your mind. Now then. For the duration of your stay here—for the rest of the month, until our regular physician in residence comes back from *his* vacation—you are going to be a rather busy man. We run into minor problems here and there, you know. Nothing to do with the drug, but peripheral things. A young lady sleeps on the balcony to her room and neglects to wear her bathing suit; that can give you a nasty burn, and it must be attended to so that she is not unhappy when she finally goes home. Or a gentleman gets pneumonia. We have two cases of that now, because of the bad weather. They'll need penicillin treatment, and whatever else you deem appropriate. After all," he said, "you're the doctor."

Clark sat calmly in his chair. He stared at Lefevre and said, "Sorry."

"Sorry?"

"Yes. Sorry. I won't play."

Lefevre frowned. "That's a rather serious decision on your part."

"Sorry."

"I strongly advise you to reconsider."

Clark shook his head. "No."

"You must realize, of course, that we have anticipated such a maneuver. We are prepared for the possibility that you would reject the plan, and begin scheming. Thinking up ways to blow the whistle on our organization, tell the world, let everyone know about the drug of choice. Eh?"

Clark kept his face expressionless, but in fact such thoughts had been running through his mind.

"We have devised a method for dealing with such plans," Lefevre said.

He pressed a button on his desk, and two waiters came into the room. They stood quietly by the door.

"I think," Lefevre said, "that a demonstration is best."

And then, almost before he knew what had happened, the two waiters grabbed him and held him, and Lefevre came forward with a gun in his hand, pressed it to Clark's arm, and fired. There was a hissing sound, and a slight pain.

"Release him."

The waiters let Clark sit down; he stopped struggling and rubbed his sore arm.

"And what was that?"

"I'm rather surprised, doctor," Lefevre said. "I would have thought you'd have guessed. We have just given you a dose of another compound. It is the reverse of the drug we give here. The exact opposite."

Clark waited, preparing himself for some sensation. Nothing happened. He felt a little queasy, but that was all.

"The posterior thalamic nuclei, on the inferior aspect,"

Lefevre said, "can produce most peculiar sensations when stimulated."

He held up the tuning fork; the metal glinted in the light. Then he swung it down abruptly, striking the table.

Clark heard a hum.

15
REVERSAL

There was no immediate change. He remained sitting in the office, staring at Lefevre, with the two men at his back. He continued to rub his arm, still sore from the pneumatic hypodermic.

Gradually, he became aware of an unearthly silence in the room, a still and muffled quality. He looked back at one of the men, and was surprised to see he was talking.

He glanced at Lefevre, who was replying to the man.

Clark heard nothing. He saw the lips move, watched as Lefevre gestured and smiled, but he heard nothing.

"It's a trick," he said aloud. "You're only pretending to talk. You're trying to frighten me."

At this, Lefevre turned to Clark and said something, shaking his head. Clark tried to read the lips but could not.

"You're trying to frighten me."

And then, he became aware that he heard nothing at all in the room. Normal sounds—feet on the carpet, the ticking of a clock on the desk, the sounds of breathing, movement, the rain outside—he heard nothing. He could not even hear the beating of his own—

"My heart," he said, and put his hand to his chest. He felt nothing. Suddenly afraid, he reached for his wrist to feel the pulse.

There was no pulse.

"My heart has stopped."

They had poisoned him. He felt a coldness creep over him, beginning in his hands and legs and ears, moving toward the center of his body. An icy, gray coldness.

"You're killing me."

The room was still silent, the men still standing and watching him. He took a deep breath, but his lungs weren't working; the air caught in his throat; he was dizzy and gasping.

They were killing him.

For a moment, he was able to sit in the chair and tell himself, *This isn't happening, it's only a drug,* and then in the next moment panic washed over him. He leapt up and scrambled for the door. The men stood and watched him as he clawed at the doorknob, his cold fingers slipping off the metal, his hands barely able to grasp and touch. He was shaking now, his body vibrating in an uncontrollable way.

He fell to his knees, weak and shaking, and leaned against the door. He felt two arms lifting him up, and setting him down in the chair once more.

Lefevre, behind the desk, lit a cigar, puffing gray smoke at Clark. Clark watched the smoke billow toward him. So that was it: poison gas. The drug was just a ruse. Actually, they were using gas.

He sniffed the air, and smelled nothing for a moment. Then he began to smell rich tobacco, and then . . . something else.

Acrid, sharp, burning.

Poison gas.

Lefevre, watching him, laughed soundlessly. Smoke curled out from his mouth as he laughed.

Clark was bathed in a cold sweat. He continued to shake

and shiver. He closed his eyes and turned away from the gas, a last, final gesture of avoidance, postponing the inevitable.

Then something new happened. He felt cool air around him, fresh and clean; he heard voices, and he stopped shaking.

When he opened his eyes, Lefevre was handing him the towel and saying, "Not bad, eh?"

Clark could not speak. He sat in the chair, weak and exhausted, gasping for breath.

"Of course," Lefevre said, "that was only a small dose. Fifteen seconds—that's all we let you go through—and even that on a small dose. You didn't even dream. And," he said, "you may be thankful for that."

He sat down behind the desk.

"However, Dr. Clark, the next time we will not use a small dose, and we will not limit the stress to fifteen seconds. I can assure you the experience will be vastly more unpleasant." He sighed.

"It is a most interesting drug, you know," he said. "In the experimental trials on monkeys and chimpanzees, we found that the animals did not survive prolonged exposure to the effects. They all killed themselves, in the most bizarre ways. One spider monkey strangled itself with its tail—very curious. You see, the drug is intolerable. A creature will do anything to be free of its influence. Anything. I think you can understand that."

"I think so," Clark said, wiping his face with the towel.

"Good. Then let us get down to business. There is a lady in room fourteen with a bad sunburn on her back. It needs attending. The gentleman in room twelve has incipient bronchopneumonia. He needs medication. The woman in . . ."

Clark listened, and when Lefevre was through, he went to work.

DRUG OF CHOICE

In the following days, he came to understand the system of the resort very well. Guests were given an initial dose of the drug in their mango punch; thereafter, it was administered as a simple white pill, taken with a glass of water. The drug was given by an attendant, who stood by, watching to be sure it was taken.

The duration of drug effect seemed to be sixteen hours, and it was remarkably constant. Dosages and schedules for each guest were charted on a large sheet at the registration desk. Nearby was another large sheet, which listed some personal information about each guest, his predominant fantasies about what was happening ("Vigorous sportsman. Has been hunting and fishing all trip." "Compulsive gambler, on big winning streak." "Spending vacation with secretary, name of Alice.") in order to guide the waiters who had to interact with the guests, from time to time.

Every second day, each guest was given a "high", meaning an episode of pleasure-coma brought on by a hum from the television set. Lefevre explained that the highs had to be spaced out, because of the intensity of the experience.

Meals were brought around three times a day to guests not on a high. They were prepared in a dingy kitchen, located behind the main building of the hotel. The food was always abominable, but it was delivered in a careful way.

The waiter would bring the tray, and set it down. He would say to the guest, "Where would you like to dine tonight?"

"Oh, the main ball dining room."

"That's where you are."

"Oh, good."

The waiter would then say, "And what would you like for dinner?"

"May I see the menu please?"

"You have it in your hand."

"Oh yes," the guest would say. "So I do." He would stare

down at his empty hands. "Now let me see . . . is your crab fresh?"

"Yes, sir."

"Then I'll have the crab. To begin, caviar. And a bottle of Dom Perignon '49."

"Very good sir. And here you are." The waiter would indicate the tray.

"Superb," the guest would say, beginning to eat. "Marvelous food, really marvelous."

Lefevre had an additional comment about the food. "You know," he said, "most of our guests lose weight during their stay here. They think they are eating heartily, and think it is excellent, but in fact they don't eat a lot. So they lose—two pounds, three pounds, five pounds. They notice it on the way home, and are invariably pleased. They think they've been so active and vigorous that the weight was lost despite their heavy eating. It is a peculiarity of our culture," he said, "that *nobody* is unhappy about losing weight."

The guests spent nearly all of their time in their rooms. On sunny days, they would be taken out to the balcony to lie in the sun and get tanned; otherwise, they were hardly bothered. Every second day a group of "fixers" would go around to each room, talking to the guests. The fixers were people who reinforced fantasies by altering the environment.

There were three fixers, a psychologist, a sociologist, and Lefevre himself. Clark went with them on their rounds one day.

They talked to one guest who said, "I made love to my wife on the beach last night and I got sand in my trousers." He chuckled. "Tore them, too."

Lefevre poured sand into the man's trouser cuffs, and tore them slightly.

"What else?"

"I had a wonderful meal last night, but I was a little tipsy. I got some shrimp sauce on my tie."

The sociologist went to the closet, found a tie, and poured catsup over it.

In the next room, a woman reported that she had gone swimming in the ocean and had forgetfully taken her watch; it was now stopped.

"So it is," Lefevre said, slipping it off her wrist and dropping it into a glass of salt water.

"You see," Lefevre said, "the fixers do this kind of minor, necessary environmental change, to correspond with guests' fantasies. In fact, the changes are easy. They tend to fall into a small range of problems—like stains on clothing, watches in salt water, and unstrung tennis rackets."

Clark nodded, remembering his own racket.

"We also provide minor scrapes and injuries to our guests. Usually local anesthetic, and then coarse sandpaper does the trick. Once in a great while, we get some guest who fantasizes an unimportant but major injury. One man thought he was badly cut by a knife while fishing. Another thought he was blinded in one eye by powder while he was hunting."

"What do you do then?"

"That," Lefevre said, "is a job for our psychologist."

The psychologist, a thin man in a sport shirt and rumpled slacks, smiled shyly. "I investigate the underlying reasons for the self-destructive fantasy. And I correct it. It can be a slow process, sometimes it takes days. That is why we counter-suggest to the guests when they first arrive—we tell them all how fabulously safe our facilities are, and how no one has ever been seriously hurt at the resort. This makes it more difficult, you see, for them to build a well-integrated fantasy of bodily harm."

"Meanwhile," Lefevre said, "our sociologist handles other

matters. When we first started this resort, we planned it as an isolated hideaway, with no communication to the outside. No telephone, no telegraph—guests couldn't communicate out, and couldn't receive messages coming in. We tried to make it work, but it wouldn't. We could convince businessmen that their business would wait, that they needn't bother with long-distance calls daily to New York or London. That was simple. But what do you do when a man's wife is seriously ill, or his business associate has died? What do you do with some major crisis?"

Clark turned to the sociologist.

"That's where I come in," the sociologist said. "I help in the process of making a guest's responses to stress appropriate. I help the guest to draft communications, letters, and cables. I help to plan the guest's early return home, and help him to deal with his guilt over a tragedy which occurred while he was off having a good time. A common situation is one where a man is off with his secretary and meantime his wife develops cancer, or has a severe auto accident, or something. The guy oozes guilt, and it is manifest in various ways, depending on his personality structure, his place in society, his education, his background, his occupation, and so forth. I help him deal with these problems within the context of his life." He smiled. "It's a lot more difficult than pouring whiskey over a cocktail dress, or catsup over a tie."

Clark said, "You seem to have thought of everything."

"Yes," Lefevre said.

The resort had a kind of fascination for Clark, it was such a grand illusion, so carefully maintained and prepared. For several days he watched the process with absorption, and did not think about the future. But eventually, he began to wonder.

His own duties were not taxing. When the storm blew over and good weather returned, the cases of pneumonia cleared quickly, and the number of sunburns was quite small. One fifty-year-old man began to develop chest pain, and was—with the help of the psychologist and the sociologist—sent home to a hospital. Otherwise, life was uneventful.

He had one bad moment with Sharon Wilder. He went to her room to check a possible eye infection; she had complained about itching eyes to one of the waiters who brought her dinner.

When he entered her room, he found her wearing a nightgown, sitting up in a chair. It was midday; she looked tanned and healthy.

"Hello," she said when he entered the room. She gave no sign of recognition.

"Hello," he said. "I am the hotel doctor."

"Oh," she said. "Good."

He went over and examined her eyes. One was red and inflamed. "Has your eye been bothering you?"

"Yes," she said. "It happened while I was sailing yesterday. I think the wind blew something in."

He turned back the lid, and found an eyelash, which he wiped away with a bit of cotton.

"Thank you," she said when he was through. "You're very gentle. I like doctors."

He nodded.

"I came here with a doctor," she said. "You know Dr. Clark?"

"Yes, I think so . . ."

"I came here with him," she said. "But I wish I hadn't."

He told himself that he ought to leave now, that he shouldn't hear more. But he stayed. "Why is that?"

"They made me do it," she said.

"Who did?"

"George, and the others."

"What others?"

"Harvey Blood, all the others."

"How do you happen to know them?"

"I've been working for them," she said, "for a long time. They control everything."

"And they made you bring Dr. Clark?"

"Yes. They have some kind of plan for him."

"A plan?"

"Yes."

"For here? At the resort?"

"Yes. But also later . . ."

"Do you know what the plan is?"

"No." She shook her head. "But I worry."

"What about?"

"Roger," she said. "I worry about him."

"Why do you worry?"

"Because he's so *stupid*," she said, and lapsed into silence.

He tried to tell himself that it meant nothing, that she was simply expressing a fantasy under the influence of a drug. He had heard other fantasies from guests which were impossible and untrue; there was no reason to believe differently about Sharon Wilder.

He tried to tell himself, to convince himself.

It didn't work.

Several days later, as his month at the resort was ending, he said to Lefevre, "I'll be going back soon."

"Yes," Lefevre said. "You will."

"To Los Angeles?"

Lefevre laughed. "Of course. That's your home, isn't it?"

Clark frowned. "But I know a lot. I know a lot about this island, and about Advance. You don't expect me to believe that you're just going to turn me loose—"

"I do expect you to believe it," Lefevre said. "That is exactly what we intend."

"You're not afraid I'll talk?"

"Talk to whom?" Lefevre said, and laughed. "Nobody would believe you if you told them the truth. They'd laugh you out of town. No, no, we're not worried."

Three days later, he was in his room, packing his suitcase and preparing to return to Los Angeles.

16
THE SHORT SAD LIE OF ROGER CLARK

"Now seriously," Sharon Wilder said, as the seaplane took off, "wasn't that the most fabulous place?"

"Fabulous," Clark said.

"I adored every minute of it," Sharon said, and snuggled up against his shoulder. "I just *loved* it."

"So did I."

She yawned. "But I'm sleepy . . . all that excitement . . ."

A few minutes later, she dozed off. Looking around the airplane, Clark saw that most of the other passengers were sleeping as well.

He did not feel sleepy at all. In fact, he was more wide-awake than he had felt in days. He checked his watch; in an hour, they would reach Nassau, and then an hour after that, Miami.

Miami, he decided, was the place. Not Los Angeles. They would almost certainly be waiting for him in Los Angeles, but they might not be expecting anything in Miami.

He tried to formulate a plan. He wouldn't have much time; it would have to be done in the airport. He could call the police—or he could go to the airport police—or perhaps the medical station at the airport, he might be believed by doctors—or he could call his lawyer in Los Angeles from the airport, and get his advice—or he could call the police, an anonymous tip to investigate Eden Island, that it was all a fraud . . .

He considered each idea in turn, and tried to make up his mind.

But two hours later, when he landed in Miami, he still had not decided.

"Harry, will you come on already, we'll miss the plane . . . Harry, do you want us to miss the plane, is that what you want, Harry?"

The woman pounded on the glass telephone booth. Inside, Harry turned his back to her. Clark, waiting in line, sighed. This had been going on for five minutes.

"Harry . . ."

Clark looked around. The booth was located along a corridor leading to the departure gates. People were walking up and down, going to planes, leaving them, family, friends, everyone . . .

He watched the crowd carefully, wondering why he was bothering. Did he expect to find someone he knew?

"Harry, Sadie is waiting for us at the airport, if we miss the plane she'll worry. Harry, do you want her to worry, your own sister, your own flesh and blood, Harry?"

Clark looked at the coins in his hand; they were slippery now with sweat. He was sweating a lot, it seemed. He looked at the coins and tried to decide who he was going to call. He hadn't made up his mind, but somehow he felt that once he was inside the booth, with the glass door closed and the receiver in his hand, he would know who to call. He would know instinctively.

"Harry, I should have to worry my hair out over a simple airplane, why do you do this to me—"

At that moment, Harry finished his call and stepped out of the booth. He turned to the woman.

"Shut up, dear," he said, and walked off.

Clark got into the booth, heart beating fast, and dropped his dime in. He heard it cling through.

He waited.

He looked down at the card attached to the bottom of the phone. It was a rate card, with numbers to call for long distance, person-to-person, emergencies, ambulance, police . . .

Police.

Dial 0.

He dialed zero. The operator answered, "Can I help you?"

"Get me the police," he said. It came out as a whisper; he hadn't intended that.

"I'm sorry, I can't hear—"

"I said, get me the police."

"Is this an emergency?"

"Of course it's an emergency," he said, turning in the narrow booth to look over his shoulder.

"Do you wish to be connected with Miami police, or Miami Beach police, or the airport police please?"

"I don't care," Clark said. "Just so you hurry—"

There was a knock on the door to the booth. He turned. Two men in trenchcoats were standing there.

"Hold on, operator."

He opened the door.

"I'm on the phone," he said.

One of the men smiled and said, "We're police officers."

That's very quick service, Clark thought, and then he

realized that it was too quick, much too quick. "I want to see your identification."

They reached into their pockets and flipped badges in little leather billfolds. He couldn't really see, but it looked—

"Are you Roger Clark?"

"Yes . . ."

"Doctor Roger Clark of Los Angeles, California?"

"Yes . . ."

The other was checking a picture and a sheet of paper. "Caucasian male, age twenty-eight, five feet ten inches, medium build—"

"I'm Roger Clark, but I don't understand—"

"Please come with us," the other police officer said. He smiled. "You're just the man we've been looking for."

"I am?" He came out of the booth reluctantly. "But why?"

"You're pretty famous, Dr. Clark. You know that, of course. Pretty darned famous."

They steered him down the corridor, one on each side.

"We've all been looking for you, you're just the man we wanted to see."

"I am?"

He must have looked alarmed, because the other man smiled reassuringly and said, "Just routine. We need your help, that's all."

"Help?"

"That's right. Just routine."

"Routine what?"

"We'll explain all that," the man said.

As they walked, Clark began to wonder. Somehow, they didn't seem like cops. They were too pleasant or something; it wasn't right. They were moving him quite rapidly down the corridor; up ahead he saw the departure gates, a flight lounge, bar . . .

He stopped.

"Wait!"

They paused, and turned to look at him. There was something pitying in their expressions, and something hesitant and careful. They smiled.

"Come along, Doctor."

"Everything will be fine, Doctor."

They took his elbows, leading him forward.

"You're not cops," Clark said.

"Sure we are," one said.

"What else would we be, Doctor?"

"I don't know," Clark said, "but I know you're not cops. You're impostors."

The two men exchanged glances.

One said, "That's all right, Doctor."

"Everything will be fine."

Clark began to struggle in their grip, but they held him tightly.

"Now, don't make a scene, Roger. Just come along quietly."

"Don't be foolish, Roger. Just take it easy now."

He struggled more fiercely; people stopped to look, to watch as he went, wriggling and twisting between the two men.

"There's no point in that, Roger," one man said soothingly.

"Just stay calm, Roger. Everything will be fine."

Abruptly, he stopped struggling. He relaxed and walked quietly between them. He had a plan.

"Much better, Roger."

"Much more comfortable, Doctor."

Ahead, clearly visible, standing by the entrance to the flight lounge, was a cop.

A real cop in a blue uniform, nightstick swinging idly in his left hand.

A cop.

Clark allowed himself to be led forward, and he said nothing until he was nearly abreast of the cop. And then he fought and shouted, "Help! Help! I'm being kidnapped! Help, police!"

He felt foolish, but he was frightened, frightened and cold in the grip of the two men. The cop in blue looked over strangely. "What's happening here?" he said to the two men.

One replied, "We're taking him in, Sam."

The cop in blue nodded. "Okay, Lieutenant." He looked closely at Clark. "Say, is this . . . ?"

"Right, Sam. It's Roger Clark."

"No kidding," Sam said, pushing his blue cap back on his head. "You found him here, huh? In Miami airport! Well, isn't that something."

One of the men leaned over. "Not really, Sam. We were tipped."

"Aaah." Sam nodded wisely.

"Come along, Roger," the men said, and steered him into the flight lounge. Clark was stunned, so astonished that he could no longer struggle. It seemed these men really were policemen after all. Unless the cop in blue was also a fake. But no, that didn't seem possible, it was too elaborate a hoax, and for no purpose . . .

He looked around the lounge. The men were taking him into the bar, which was dark and noisy; he was led to a corner. In the darkness he could barely see two people, sitting at a far table. As he came closer, he could begin to make out their features—

"Ah, officers," Harvey Blood said, rising. "You found him. Excellent work."

And standing beside him, George Washington said again, "Excellent, excellent."

Clark stared at them, and then over at the two cops. If they were cops.

"How is he?" Harvey Blood asked.

"A little excitable, but pretty good."

"Oh, excitable. We can fix that." Harvey Blood turned to Washington. "It wouldn't do to have him excited on the airplane. Jumping around, disturbing the other passengers . . ."

"No," Washington said, reaching to the floor, bringing up a black physician's bag, opening it on the bar table.

"No," agreed the two men, watching as Washington removed a syringe, filled it, held it to the light.

"Listen," Clark said, finding his voice at last. "This is all some kind of mistake. I know these two men. They are Harvey Blood and George Washington. They—"

"We know Dr. Blood and Dr. Washington," one man said calmly. "We know all about everything. You know, we've been following you in the bulletins for days. Never thought we'd see you here, though."

"Bulletins?"

One of the men asked Blood, "How'd you know he was going to be here?"

"Someone in Nassau spotted him," Blood said.

"Nassau! How'd he get down there?"

"We traced him from Los Angeles," Blood said. "Found the girl who sold him the ticket. He flew to Nassau five days ago."

"Pretty tricky," the man said, looking at Clark and shaking his head. "Pretty clever."

Washington took Clark's arm, held it out, rolled up the sleeve. Clark began to struggle just as he felt the coolness of the alcohol swab.

"You can't do this—"

The needle stung.

"—to me, you can't do this."

Another swab of alcohol. His sleeve was rolled down.

"He'll be fine now," Harvey Blood said. "Just fine."

PART III
MADNESS

*"It is indeed harmful to come under the sway
of utterly new and strange doctrines."*
SAYING OF CONFUCIUS

17
THE SCIENTIFIC COMING

He heard a sound like the roar of a huge forest fire, and he smelled smoke. The sound was very loud, deafening, but somehow familiar at the same time.

He opened his eyes, and looked to the direction of the sound. He was lying on a couch, fully dressed, in some kind of office. There was a window to his right. He got up slowly and walked over to look out.

Traffic.

A freeway, thick with automobiles. Yellow-gray sky and faint, diffuse sunlight.

"Los Angeles," he said, and shook his head. He didn't remember what had happened. There was something about boarding an airplane, and later, being met at the airport by a limousine—

"My God, you look awful," Harvey Blood said.

Clark turned. Blood was standing just inside the door.

"You're . . . you're an absolute *mess*," Blood said, gesturing to Clark's clothes. "You can't go like that."

He came up and pushed Clark into a chair.

"No, that would ruin everything," he said. "Just a minute."

He went to the door, and came back with two girls. One began to comb Clark's hair while the other shaved him with an electric razor. A boy came in with a suit on a hanger, a fresh shirt, and a tie; he hung it on the back of the door and walked out. Blood stood in the center of the room and watched the girls working on Clark.

"Hurry it up, girls," he said. "We're behind schedule already."

Clark said, "Behind schedule for what?"

"The audition," Blood said.

"What audition?"

"For Project GG," he said. "The Angela Sweet mockup."

Clark said nothing. He didn't understand what Blood was talking about.

Blood seemed to realize this. "It's all strange at first," he said. "And of course you're tired from your journey. But that will pass."

Clark said, "Where are we?"

"Advance. We landed in LA last night. Do you remember that?"

"No, not really."

"Well, it went very smoothly. Let's go, girls."

The girls finished and stepped back. Clark stood; they helped him out of his clothing, and handed him the clean clothes. He dressed slowly.

"Clark, come on, come on," Blood said.

Roger Clark knotted his tie as slowly as he could.

"Look," Blood said. "This kind of funny business won't go. You'd better understand that. You're in trouble and you need me."

"I do?"

"You're damned right you do. Now hurry it up."

Walking down the steps to the waiting limousine, Clark said, "Why do I need you?"

"Because you're in trouble."

"What kind of trouble?"

Harvey Blood glanced at his watch and entered the limousine. Clark followed him; two men were already there, sitting on the little fold-down seats. They had charts and briefcases opened, papers out.

The limousine started off.

Clark said, "What kind of trouble?"

"Later," Blood said. He turned to the two men.

"We've got it down to twenty, Harvey," one said. "They're a pretty good group." He laughed. "Some of them can even sing."

"The hell with that," Blood said. He looked at the other.

"Psychological testing is completed," the man said. "On all twenty finalists. The correlation with somatotyping of body form is quite precise. You've got a split into two basic groups, really. What we call the projection-affective group, with high raw scores on scales twelve, delta, and nine. Then there's the ego-flexor group, which scored high on scales five, beta, and two. It's hard to say which would be the better choice."

"I see," Blood nodded.

The first man said, "We've got standardized costumes waiting, and the pattern is set. All it requires is your final decision."

"How about the costume for GG?"

"We have a preliminary model. All the girls will wear it. The plastics people have just finished wiring them."

"Fine. And the sound?"

"We'll go there afterward. The mixing studios are doing fine work, I think you'll agree. And the boys are coming together nicely."

Blood nodded and sat back. The second man handed him

a sheaf of graphs, with points plotted on peculiar circular axes. It was a kind of graph Clark had never seen before.

There were also several pages of photographs, but they were also peculiar. One page was the faces of twenty girls, but the other pages were isolated photos of legs, elbows, shoulders, feet. Each page was stamped: "PROJECT GLOW."

"What's that?" Clark said.

"Shut up," Harvey Blood said. "I'm thinking."

An auditorium, empty, the rows of wooden seats stretching back into darkness. In front of them, a bare and lighted stage.

Harvey Blood slumped down in the front row and looked up at the stage. The two men sat on either side of him; Clark sat next to one of them.

Nobody said anything, but after a moment, a man in a dark suit came onto the stage, carrying a microphone on a heavy base. He set the microphone down in the middle of the stage, right in front of Blood.

"Are you ready now, sir?" he asked.

"Ready," Blood said. He took out a pair of glasses, wiped them on his tie, and put them on. He folded his hands across his chest and looked up expectantly.

"There are three runs," one of the men said, leaning over to Clark. "Dr. Blood can eliminate at any time. Do you understand?"

"No," Clark said.

"You'll get the hang of it, after a while," the man said.

The stage lights went down. A voice said, "Number one," and a girl walked out. She was tall and slender, with dark hair and a gentle face. She wore black slacks and a frilly white blouse.

"You see," one of the men whispered to Clark, "on the first

run, the girls wear whatever they want. The next two runs are standardized. But this run is important to personality projection and affect penetrance."

"Oh."

The girl walked slowly across the stage, oblivious to the men in the front row. She reached the opposite side, turned, and walked back. Clark looked over to see what Blood was doing. He was frowning.

Blood said, "Why slacks?"

"Ego interference," one man said. "Subconscious withdrawal complex. She relies on conveyed fragility."

Blood continued to frown. "Cut her."

The aide picked up a small hand walkie-talkie. "Cut one," he said.

There was a pause, and then a voice said, "Number two," and a second girl walked across the stage. This one was short, with large breasts and hips, and a pert face. She wore a mini-skirt and sweater.

"Projection-affective," one of the men whispered. "Written all over her."

"Oh," Clark said.

This girl Blood seemed to like. He smiled slightly, and said nothing. The girl walked off the stage and a third one came on, a dark-haired girl in a leather skirt, vest, boots.

"Strangely enough, this one is ego-flexor, though she doesn't look it."

Clark leaned over to see Blood's reaction, but his face was enigmatic.

The fourth girl wore a jumper; she had large breasts and blond hair.

"Look at the way she walks," Blood said. "Terrible. Cut her."

And so it went, through all twenty girls. Clark tried to make sense of what was happening, but he could not. Every once in a while, one of the men would lean over to explain things, but the explanations never helped. About all he understood was that they were selecting a girl.

For something.

At the end of the first run, Blood said, "How many?"

"Thirteen left."

"All right. Let's get on with it."

The new sequence began, this time starting with number two, since number one was eliminated. Number two wore a brief black bikini. She had not taken two steps onto the stage before Blood hissed: "She has a scar!"

"Yes," one of the men said, "appendix . . ."

"You knew that? And you kept her? That's absurd."

"We thought perhaps it would increase identification, help in the human element, a girl with a—"

"A *scar*?" Blood shuddered. "Never. Glow Girl can't have a scar. Cut her."

Over the walkie-talkie: "Cut number two."

The next girl came out, in an identical bikini. Clark watched her, but he was rapidly losing interest. In his mind, the girls began to merge; he lost the ability to differentiate them. He found himself listening to Blood's comments.

On number five: "Bad hips. Awkward in the hips. Cut her."

Number seven: "Terrible breasts. And she doesn't *move* right. Cut her."

Number eleven: "Ugh! Cut her."

Number fourteen: "Too shy. She comes over shy. Cut her."

Number nineteen: "That's brazen. It's flaunting: cut her."

Number twenty: "She acts tired. Cut her."

At the end of the run, he said again, "How many?"

"Six."

Blood sighed. "Still six? Hell. All right."

He sat back and waited for the third run. Five minutes passed before the first of the girls came onstage. She wore a strange dress, made of plastic squares, loose. But the plastic, Clark saw, was glowing. The dress moved gently with the girl, glowing bright pink.

Blood smiled. "Very nice. Where are the batteries?"

"In the collar. Mercury-cadmium."

"Very nice."

Another girl came on, before the first had left, and then another, until all six were lined up on the stage. Each wore the same glowing dress of plastic.

Blood looked from one to the next. He was frowning hard. He said, "Let's hear the one on the far right."

"Far right," one of the men shouted.

The girl on the far right, a redhead, seemed surprised at first, and then pleased. She walked up to the microphone, skirt moving gently, and said, "My name is Angela Sweet. I'm the Glow Girl. Nice to meet you."

"Hmmm," Blood said. "Try the third from the left."

"Third from the left!"

Another girl walked up to the microphone and said, "My name is Angela Sweet. I'm the Glow Girl. Nice to meet you."

This was repeated until finally the last girl said, "My name is Angela Sweet. I'm the Glow Girl, and I wish I knew what the hell I'm doing here."

There was nervous laughter from all the girls.

Blood smiled.

Then, without taking his eyes off the line of girls, he said, "Clark, what's your decision?"

"My what?"

"Decision. Which one do you pick?"

"I don't know. I don't even know what you're picking them for."

"That doesn't matter," Blood said. "Choose."

"But why me? I don't—"

"Listen," Blood said, "do you think we brought you down here for the ride? Choose!"

Clark hesitated. He looked at the girls. Finally he said, "Second from the left."

"Second from the left," Blood repeated, nodding.

"Second from the left," the man said into the walkie-talkie.

Blood stood. "That's that," he said, and walked out of the auditorium. The others followed, Clark last of all. He was stunned. He looked back to the stage; the girls were clustered together, talking. The one he had chosen was a dark-haired girl with large eyes.

Up ahead, by the door, Blood shouted, "Come on, Clark, we haven't got all day."

Clark hurried up the aisle, away from the stage.

Surrounded by electronic equipment, dials, and switches, they sat in the soundproofed room and looked through the glass at the group in the inner room. Five young men with long hair, guitars, drums, an organ.

Blood stared at them, and placed earphones over his head. "Let's hear them."

At a signal, the group started to play. One of the other men leaned over to Clark.

"This is the group, the backup," he said. "The Scientific Coming. We've finally got them polished into some kind of shape, but it was a battle, I can tell you. This first cut is a standard."

He handed Clark a set of earphones. Electronic sound blasted him. As he listened, somebody handed him a sheet of words:

SHOCK TREATMENT

My little analeptic
She meets me at the door.
Gives me a kiss,
And I'm rolling on the floor.
In shock treatment,
Shock treatment,
Shock treatment,

Rolling on the floor . . . or . . . or . . .
Blow my mind,
In a catatonic fit,
Losing my cool,
But loving it.
In shock treatment,
Stock treatment,
Block treatment,
But loving it . . . it . . . it . . .

Gotta admit,
It's really a show.
Wears me out,
And leaves me kinda low.
From shock treatment,
Rock treatment,

Mock treatment,
Leaves me really low . . . low . . . ow . . .

The song was finished. Clark took off the earphones. "Nothing special," he was told. "They're just warming up. This next is a very sensitive ballad, very now, very today."
Clark put the headphones back on.

SICKIE, SICKIE

Sickie, sickie, where you goin'?
All day long, and night time glowin'.
There you go,
Poppin' pills.
Seeking out,
Those extra thrills.
Don't you know,
It's really here.
Can't you see,
It's only fear.

Sickie, sickie, where you goin'?
All day long, and night time glowin'.
Out of sight
Mind a fog.
Big machine
A little cog.
Don't you know,
It can't be done.
You must see,
That you're the one.

*Pick you up,
Or put you down.
Start you high,
Or crash you down.
We don't care
It's what you do
But you know
We're really true.*

"Doesn't that grab you?" someone asked Clark. "Here, check this out."

He was handed an album cover: SIX INCH INCISION. Glow Girl and the Scientific Coming. The cover photo showed the group of hairy young men in the other room, but there was a blank space—for Glow Girl, he presumed. He turned the album over to look at the song titles.

"These are just tentative, of course," he was told. "We may still call the album *Acid Fast*. The song titles are tentative as well. *Molecular Love*, for instance, may be changed to *Cryin' Ions Over You*."

Harvey Blood looked over at Clark, obviously relishing his confusion.

"You see the general principle," he said. "Science. Everyone is afraid of science. Terrified of it. And yet fascinated by it at the same time. We're bringing science down to the masses, making it agreeable, understandable. We're *educating* people."

"Oh," Clark said.

"Now, all that remains," Blood said, "is to make our new creation palatable to the public. In fact, enthusiastically received. There are slightly more than seventy rock groups which are, in any sense of the word, big-time. Of those, perhaps ten are really important. We intend to beat them all. The Beatles, the Stones, the Airplane, the Cream, Traffic, Jimi Hendrix, the Chambers Brothers—we are going to put them all out of business."

"I see."

"You doubt me. You shouldn't. After all, look what we did with a product as untalented and basically boring as Sharon Wilder, the former Alice Blankfurt?"

Harvey Blood laughed.

"Isn't science wonderful?" he said.

18
GLOW GIRL

"You see," Harvey Blood said, as they drove back in the limousine, "the true purpose of Advance is the harnessing of science to turn a comfortable commercial profit. The drug of choice is just one example. Our use of it to operate a resort hotel may seem strange at first, but think about it. It's wholly logical. In the same way, the Glow Girl will utilize advances—"

"What about Sharon Wilder? What scientific advance does she represent?"

Blood chuckled. "Applied psychology. We had it all worked out in advance—what she should look like, how she should act, what kinds of things she should talk about, what kind of photographs she should pose for, what kind of movies she should appear in. It was a careful balance, designed to fulfill the nationwide expectations for a modern sex symbol. I think you will grant," he said, "that we've succeeded handsomely."

"And the Glow Girl?"

"Ah. Now that is an interesting matter. Those inane songs

you listened to are actually quite carefully prepared. The rhythm is timed as multiples of brain-wave frequency and function. If played loudly it can have quite a hypnotic effect. This, combined with the image of the Glow Girl, the scientific-sexual overtones of the group—"

"Scientific-sexual?"

"Of course. But Advance is not stopping there. We are already engaged in the manufacture of a new line of perfumes for women, and cologne for men. We are planning the introduction of a new game which will, we predict, replace professional football as the most interesting game in America. We have a new contraceptive device which needs to be taken only once a year—a great boon for teenagers trying to hide nasty facts from their parents. Very shortly, we will begin marketing three-dimensional television. And finally, we have reason to believe that we are on the track of a mild viral illness which increases sexual potency."

"I don't believe you," Clark said, but he really did.

"In time," Harvey Blood said, "you will come around to our way of thinking. I don't need to tell you that we are not a unique corporation in this country. We are merely a little smarter, a little faster than the others. But other firms are springing up, all across America. This is the way of the future—research and development, and commercial application on an imaginative basis."

Clark said, "What about me? Why did you involve me in all this?"

"We needed you."

"For what? To pick the Glow Girl?"

"Oh no. That was just a minor thing. We've had major plans for you, right from the start."

"You mean for the island?"

"Well, no. Other things."

"Like what?"

"We expect," Blood said, "to utilize your knowledge of drugs and testing." He held up his hand. "And please, no tiresome stories of how you will resist us, and refuse us, and fight us. We can make you do it, and if you are wise you will go along willingly. After all, we can make you a rich man."

The limousine pulled up in front of the Advance building. As they got out, Blood looked at his watch and said, "Behind schedule again. You're late for your appointment."

"My appointment?"

"Yes. With the Glow Girl."

"And what am I supposed to do with her?"

"Examine her, of course," Blood said. "You're a doctor; we want a full report on the physical fitness of our girl. After all," he said, "we're going to be putting a lot of time, effort, and money into her. A hell of a lot."

There was a room, a desk, an examining couch, and a nurse. The girl, wearing a simple skirt and blouse now, sat in a chair facing the desk. She looked back over her shoulder as he came in.

The nurse was matronly and forbidding. He said, "You can leave now. I'll call you when I need you."

"A nurse should be in attendance—"

"Get out," Clark said quietly, "or I'll kick you out."

"But Dr. Clark—"

"I'll worry about Blood, if that's the problem. Besides," he said, "the room is bugged."

The nurse glared at him, but left. Clark walked around

behind the desk and sat down. Immediately, he began going through the drawers. The girl watched him silently.

"My name," he said, "is Roger Clark. I'm a doctor."

The girl nodded and said nothing. She watched him as he shuffled papers, and poked among the flowers in the vase on the desk. He had no idea what he was looking for: in movies, it was small and black, with wires.

"I'm sorry," he said, continuing his search, slamming the drawers, "but I don't know your name."

"Susan Ryle. With a Y. And I wanted to thank you."

"Thank me?"

He lifted the dictaphone and peered underneath, then checked the telephone.

"Yes," she said. "For choosing me. I saw you do it, down there in the front row."

"Ummm," Clark said. "I can't find it."

"Find what?"

"The microphone. I know there's one here someplace."

"But why would there be a microphone—"

"Because this is a very personal sort of corporation," Clark said. "They take a personal interest in their employees."

"I like that," Susan Ryle said. She smiled. She had a lot of even white teeth. Close up, her eyes were dark and enormous.

"Do you? It gets a little wearing."

"The only thing is," she said, sitting back and crossing her legs, "I don't really know what I was hired for."

"You were hired to be the Glow Girl."

"Yes, but what's that?"

"The Glow Girl is a rock and roll singer. You have a group called the Scientific Coming."

"A rock and roll singer! But I can't sing a note—"

"They'll take care of that," Clark said. "They take care of

everything. And you'll make a lot of money. A well-paid employee is a contented employee."

"Yes," Susan Ryle said, but she was frowning. Still thinking about her singing ability. It occurred to Clark that she might not be over-intelligent.

"I suppose they'll give me voice lessons," she said.

"I suppose."

"In a way, it's exciting."

"I suppose."

"Don't you agree it's exciting?"

"Frankly," he said, "no. I think it's frightening, I think it's terrifying, but I do not think it is exciting."

"Oh," she said. "But aren't you an employee?"

"I'm well looked after," Clark said.

She was silent. He could tell he had confused her, and she had been confused enough at the outset. It wasn't really fair, taking out his frustration on her.

"Listen," he said. "As a doctor, I have a piece of advice."

"Yes?"

"Get out. Get out of the whole thing, right now. Forget the dough, the fame, the bright lights, and the limousine pulling up for opening night—"

"What?" She was staring at him.

He threw up his hands. "Just forget the whole damned thing. You're a nice girl. You'll make some lucky guys a fine wife. Go out, get married, get divorced, get married again, have some kids, get divorced—do the California thing, and be happy."

"You're very peculiar," she said, looking at him and tugging down at her short skirt.

"I was born under an unlucky star," Clark said.

"Gee," she said. "That's too bad."

Clark sighed. She was innocent and wide-eyed and lovely. And he would never in a million years make her understand.

He went to the door. "Nurse!"

The examination was brief. The girl was in excellent shape physically. Excellent shape.

He reported to Blood.

"That's very reassuring to hear," Blood said.

"She's a little dumb, of course—"

"Very reassuring," Blood nodded.

"And you'll have a lot of work to do, whipping her into some kind of shape as a singer—"

"We are prepared," he said mildly, "to work."

"I'm not," Clark said.

Blood seemed surprised. "I thought we'd been all over this. I thought you had come to understand."

"What I understand," Clark said, "is that a month ago I was a happy doctor working in a happy hospital. I had never heard of blue urine, or comas, or Eden Island. I had never heard of this damned corporation, or Sharon Wilder, or the Glow-Glow Girl."

"That's quite clever. We may use that."

"I had never heard of calling the police in the Miami airport, or being abducted, or held a prisoner in the middle of goddamned Santa Monica. And I want out."

Blood shrugged. "You can't get out, I'm afraid."

"I can try."

"Oh yes, of course you can try. And you may even succeed, for a few hours. But not for long. We'd have you back in no time. You see, Roger, you're with us now. Outside of here, beyond these walls, you're *nothing*. Nothing at all. There is nowhere that you could turn to, nowhere that you could go. Your old friends would shun you. They aren't your friends anymore. Your old world would reject you—it isn't your world anymore. You're with *us* now."

"The hell I am."

Blood regarded him steadily for several moments. "I can see that you're serious. I'm sorry."

"Don't be sorry."

"But I am. I hate to use you in this way. I really do. I think it's a waste of a fine mind. But at the same time, I'm grateful for the opportunity you present. I must admit it was George who thought of it first, but the fact remains, you're a fine opportunity for us, Roger. You are ideal."

He picked up a telephone on a small table behind his desk. "Get me section seven," he said.

While he was waiting, telephone cradled in his shoulder, he said, "They'll all be delighted. They're a little like vultures, actually. Hovering about waiting for their chance. And now they have it."

He spoke into the phone. "George? Set up the series right away. Yes . . . yes, I'm afraid so."

He hung up.

"You see, Roger, we can use a man of your talents in many ways. We can use you to help us, to work with us, to prepare our projects and ventures. Or we can use you in other ways. After all, look at your qualifications. You are a trained physician. You have a working knowledge of anatomy, pharmacology, biochemistry. You are experienced in biological matters, and you are a trained observer. All invaluable traits."

"Invaluable traits for what?"

"For an experimental subject, of course."

Behind him, the door opened. Two guards came in, and caught him by the arms.

Harvey Blood stood. "I think you'll find it interesting, Roger."

The guards took him out of the room.

19
K PUPPY

"Good, good," George Washington said. "Good, good, good."

He bent over Clark, securing the leather straps which held him to the wooden chair. They were in a laboratory and the chair was on some kind of metal track, which ran forward to a door in the far wall.

"We can observe you," Washington said, "by remote control. I want you to know we've taken every safeguard."

"That's reassuring."

"I feel," Washington said, tightening one of the arm straps, "that you should know a little about this series. There are no drugs involved. None at all. Instead, we are working on the K principle."

"It being?"

"Roger, you're so hostile. Try to look at it as an interesting experience. The K principle was first elaborated in Montreal. Researchers there experimented with puppies, raised from birth in zero sensory environments. They were kept in total darkness, constant temperature, constant sound for six weeks after birth. And then they were brought out into the real world."

"And they went mad."

"No. No indeed. But they acted quite peculiarly. They could see, for example; their eyes reacted to light and so forth. But they couldn't organize visual information. They walked right into walls—that kind of thing. They couldn't understand what sensory stimuli *meant*."

"That's nice."

"Meantime," George continued, "some people in Ann Arbor were experimenting with sensory deprivation in human beings. Put a person in a room with cardboard tubes on his arms and legs—so he can't feel—and a blindfold over his eyes—so he can't see—and earplugs—so he can't hear. And leave him there for a while. The subjects acted pretty strangely after a few hours.

"But the experiments were inconclusive. There was some suggestion of increased pliability, of agreeability, after exposure. Our small experiments here have tended to confirm that. But the factor of education is major, and nobody knows how to deal with that. Also, there is a question about the duration of effect. With drugs, we know that suggestibility is strictly limited. The drug wears off, and you go back to normal. But with the K principle—"

"I see," Clark said. "No wonder you're interested."

"As a scientific development, it has possibilities," Washington said. "But now we have you. Ideal subject—you're educated, informed, aware. And you know exactly what we're going to do to you."

"You're going to make me a K puppy."

"Ha ha," Washington said, and signaled to one of the technicians. The far door was opened; beyond, he could see a small room, yellowish, with strange walls.

His chair moved forward on the track.

"Enjoy yourself," Washington said.

The chair moved through the door, and into the room. The door was closed behind him. It shut with a soft, leathery sound.

A very strange sound.

And suddenly, he knew. He looked down: his chair was still on tracks, but suspended in the middle of the room, equidistant from all walls, ceiling, and floor. And every wall was the same, with strange baffles and projections.

A sound-killing room.

"Hello," he said. His voice was odd, muffled and unfamiliar to him.

"I'm in a soundproofed room," he said. He shouted it, but it came out as little more than a whisper. A soft, dull whisper.

He sat and waited. Nothing happened. He continued to sit in the chair for what seemed like a very long time; how long, he could not be sure. Perhaps five minutes, perhaps half an hour.

Then white smoke began to hiss softly into the room. It was a funny kind of smoke, opaque and totally odorless. He thought it would make him cough, but it did not.

Soon he was surrounded by white smoke, so dense that he could not see the walls. It was as if he were floating in the center of a cloud.

He remained that way for a long time. And then the sound began. It was a bizarre sound, like radio static, and maddening.

White sound.

That was what they called it: a mixture of frequencies of sound, just as white light was a mixture of wavelengths of light. It was a steady, monotonous, unvarying crackling.

White sound.

He spoke. He could hear nothing but the static, his words were lost in it, disappearing into the blanket of sound.

Very neat, he thought. White light, white sound, floating

in a foggy cloud. No up, no down, no stimuli. Nothing to look at, nothing to listen to, nothing to smell or feel.

But there was something to feel—he ran his fingers over the wooden arms of the chair. He tensed his arms against the straps until it hurt. He forced himself to pay attention to the sensations in his hands.

He continued to do this for a long time. But then, when next he noticed, his hands and legs were free; someone had taken away the straps.

He must have slept.

But he didn't remember.

He thought of getting out of the chair, of moving around, but he was afraid to move in the white fog and the white sound which came to him evenly in all directions. He was lost. He told himself that he was in a little room, that outside was a laboratory, and people checking on him, that there was a door outside to the laboratory, and that door was right ahead of him.

Ahead?

No, behind.

Behind where? What if they had turned him around when they removed the straps? What if they had changed his orientation?

He sighed. Perhaps they had, perhaps not. In any case, it was too much trouble. Too much trouble to bother with. He closed his eyes and tried to relax. There was no point in keeping them open: there was nothing to look at.

He tried to relax.

The first electric shock traveled up his spine, snapping him awake and instantly alert. He blinked his eyes. The fog was still there, and the sound.

What were they doing?

There were more shocks, and still more. He sat limply in the chair, not understanding. Sensory deprivation meant absence of sensation. By shocking him, they were providing stimuli.

Why?

He closed his eyes. He was feeling very tired now. He ran his fingers through his hair, and touched—

Wires.

Wires?

Someone had put wires on his head, he thought sleepily. That was strange of them.

Shocks again. He was sleepy in a way he had never been before; after each shock came, he dozed off immediately afterward. His bones ached and his eyes hurt with fatigue.

Another shock.

Why?

And then he realized that they were keeping him awake, purposely keeping him awake, and the electrodes on his head were connected to an encephalograph.

So they would know when he was dreaming.

Vaguely, he remembered the studies. In sleeping, a normal person dreamed with great regularity ten minutes out of every hour. If you missed a night of sleep, you dreamed twice as much the next night.

If you were awakened each time you started to dream—as indicated by changes in brain wave activity—then the sleep did you no good. You could be awakened during non-dreaming periods without harm. But if you were prevented from dreaming . . .

Another shock.

He responded sluggishly. Psychosis, that was what it produced. Sleep deprivation psychosis. The absence of dreaming drove a man—

Shock.

Mad. Drove him mad.

He had never been so tired. No one in the history of the world had been so tired. There was no greater blessing than sleep, it was better than cold mountain water, better than caviar, better than Hogarth's mother.

Hogarth's mother?

Rocking herself to sleep.

There was another shock.

He saw it all very clearly now, despite the white fog and the white sound and the shocks. He saw that the elephant king had overcome the giants in the land of Peruvian Green, and the queen of the homeostasis had integrated all the megafunctions on the top of her crystal blackboard. Meanwhile the gun was pointed at the cap of the archduke who flew over the castle tops wearing his pink beret while he selected a suitable tree upon which to perch and lay his nest of eggs. That was to be expected since there was Dante's voyage across the seven seas in glorious meritocracy and seaside playpens of laughing infants who played in the seaside digging sandcastles and innovating in the ocean before they were finally allowed to sleep, and then they were happy and gurgling, and soft voices of their dear departed mother would whisper into their ear, all sorts of marvelous reassurances about the future of the Holy Grail and IBM lost ten points in heavy low rubberneck.

Forester, a rubber of whist, eh? And then we fixed on the fort, all guns blazing for her majesty.

Eh?

20
EIGHTEENTH NERVOUS BREAKDOWN

"You'll be pleased to know," George Washington said, smiling kindly, "that everything was a complete success. An unqualified success."

Clark felt a surging thrill, a moment of great pleasure. "That's wonderful."

"We're still concerned about how long the effects will last—"

Oh dear, Clark thought, suddenly worried.

"—but we can hope, at least, that they are permanent."

Permanent? How delightful that was, how thrilling. They were truly on the verge of a breakthrough in science. He felt an almost palpable sense of discovery. It was very exciting, working here in Advance. It was the most exciting thing a young man could do.

"I'm very eager to begin work," Clark said, rubbing his hands together.

Washington gave him a funny look.

"Is something wrong, George?"

"No," George said. "It's just . . . well, sometimes I can't believe it myself, is all. You're a new man, Roger."

"I know it. I feel like a new man."

"Yes, I'm sure you must," Washington said. "Well then: down to business, eh? I'll show you around your lab, and then you can get right to work. Oh, by the way, Harvey wants to see you."

"Harvey wants to see me?" It was an honor, the president of such a fine company wanting to see him.

"Yes," George said. "Come along."

Roger met with Harvey and George in the big office. They were both very happy, and Roger felt happy as well. He was extremely eager to begin his work; he could hardly contain his excitement. It was such a wonderful company, so dynamic and interesting.

After that, George took him to the lab, which was ideally equipped, everything a man could ask for. And a smashingly beautiful technician who seemed very interested in him. They showed him where everything was stored, including the two vials of powder, one white, the other pink.

"Now then," George said, his voice ringing with enthusiasm, "these are the drugs you'll be working with. The drug of choice here"—he raised the white vial—"and the reversal drug here." He held out the pink vial. "You've had some experience with these before, so you know how vital and important this work is."

There was no question of it in Roger's mind. It was not only important, it was fascinating. It presented a huge intellectual challenge, a great stimulus.

"What we need to know," George said, "is maximum dosages for these drugs. We've been using them cautiously, because we don't know upper limits. But we suspect that we are not getting the maximum benefits from the drug administration. That's where you come in. We want you to set those limits of dosage. You'll work with animals at first, and later, when you've done the groundwork, with people."

It was thrilling, Roger thought. In his mind, he could see the endless experiments he would perform, and his steady progress toward an eventual solution to this fascinating project.

"Just one word of caution," George said. "These drugs are both very potent, and very valuable. Manufacture is still expensive, and there is only one person who does it."

"Only one?"

"Yes. Harvey. He's the only one that knows the formula, and he won't tell anyone else."

That seemed strange to Roger at first, but as he thought about it, he could understand the reasons. Harvey was being careful; he ought to be careful. Those drugs could be dangerous in the wrong hands. They could be . . . well, *exploited*.

"You see, Roger, this firm is making all its money at the present time from this drug, and its use on the island. Funds from that are financing all the research in this large building, and all our projects, like Sharon Wilder and the Glow Girl."

Roger nodded. Two excellent projects. Nice young girls given a chance in a lifetime to make good. Very worthy and charitable projects.

"So Harvey is playing it close. And he limits the amount of drug he is making available. So don't drop it or lose it or anything."

"Oh no," Roger said. "I wouldn't do anything like that." George gave him a funny look again, then smiled, and left.

The lab technician said, "We're going to have a fine time here," and Roger could only agree. Immediately, he began work.

The next two weeks were the happiest he had ever known. He had a worthy project, and he devoted himself to it during every waking hour. He lived in a pleasant room on the top floor of the building, so it was very convenient. He was close to his work and had no need to leave for anything. Whatever he requested was brought to him instantly. It was a very agreeable place to work.

He saw Sharon Wilder once, and she seemed happy to see him. She asked how things were going and he said they were going wonderfully.

During the second week, he saw Susan Ryle, the Glow Girl. She looked surprisingly different. They had done things to her, cut her hair and changed the way she made up her eyes. She was like a different person. She remarked to Roger that he looked different, too. He was very flattered.

Toward the end of the second week, he began having dreams. At first, they occurred only occasionally, strange and annoying dreams. They disturbed his sleep.

He thought of mentioning them to George, but never did. He was afraid that George would take him off the project if he knew. After all, they couldn't have an unstable man working on an important project.

And he was feeling a little unstable.

Later, the dreams began to come every night. They were always the same. He was flying an airplane over tropical islands, shining in blue water. He was happy, flying the airplane. And then the airplane would go into a dense fog, and it would start to worry him.

He would wake up in a cold sweat.

Perhaps, he thought, I am working too hard. He took more of an interest in his lab technician, who was interested in him as well. She began to spend nights in his room, and he dreamed less when she was there.

But with time, the dreams progressed. He would fly into

the fog, and then somehow he would know that there was an end to the fog, a frightening end. Something outside the comforting, frightening white fog.

He no longer invited the technician to stay with him. He was afraid that he would talk in his sleep, and she would report him to George, and that would mean he would be taken off the project. He couldn't allow that to happen. Because he lived for that project; it meant everything to him.

Everything.

Sometime during the sixth week, his dreams broke through the fog. He saw what lay beyond, and it was some kind of hideous chair.

Immediately, he woke up. He was shivering and sweating, and angry. He did not understand precisely why, but he was very, very angry.

He got out of bed in a silent rage, and dressed. He had no real idea what he was doing, or where he was going. Once dressed, he looked around the room and saw a large paperweight on his desk. It was heavy plastic, with a piece of rock embedded inside.

He carried it downstairs with him. As he moved quietly through the halls, his anger was very great; he could hardly wait until he met that damned guard.

As he reached the ground floor, he saw the guard. It was Sam, the night-duty man; Roger had met him before in the evenings.

"Hello, Dr. Clark," Sam said. "Another late night with the experiments?"

"Yes," Roger said. "Looks like it."

He let the guard walk past him. Then he turned, and swung with the paperweight. He felt a flash of horror as the heavy plastic struck skull and scalp; the guard fell and bled profusely.

His anger began to die.

The chair, he thought, and it slowly came back to him. Not all of it, but some.

Enough.

Quickly, he took the keychain from Sam's belt and used it to shut down the alarm. Then he unlocked the front door and went down the steps into the night. Two cars were parked in the lot—a black limousine and a brown sedan, which he guessed was Sam's car. He tried the keys until he found the one which unlocked the door; he got in and started the engine, and drove down the drive.

It was not until he was on the road that he realized he had no idea where he was going.

It was difficult to think clearly. Images were flashing through his mind, conflicting images.

"They did something to me," he said aloud. "They did something to my head."

That was it.

They had done something.

And now where?

Dimly, he remembered bits of conversation.

". . . you're nothing outside . . ."

"Nowhere to go . . ."

"Friends aren't friends, anymore . . ."

Was it true?

He wondered.

And then, not knowing what else to do, he drove back to his old apartment.

It was foolish of him. He should have known it would be watched. When he pulled up across the street from the entrance, he saw the man sitting in the car, and the other man lounging against a lamppost on the street corner.

By now, they would know he had escaped. They would be after him. Where could he go?

The police.

But somehow he wasn't ready to go to the police, not yet. He wanted to talk it over with somebody else, to try out the story, see how it sounded.

Sharon?

No. She'd turn him in.

Harry, the intern?

No. He would be all confused, bewildered, unhelpful.

Dr. Shine?

Perhaps. That was a good possibility. Or Dr. Andrews, the Chief of Medicine at the hospital. But somehow . . .

Janice Connor.

Of course! He snapped his fingers. Janice would hear him out.

He drove away from his apartment, toward the Strip, and parked at an all-night drive-in. The kids were there, laughing and necking in convertibles under the lights. He found a payphone near the restrooms, dropped in his money, and dialed.

A sleepy girl answered. "Hello?"

"Janice Connor, please."

"This is she."

"Janice, this is Roger Clark."

For a moment, there was silence. Then: "Who?"

"Roger Clark. You remember me, I'm the doctor—"

"Yes, yes. I remember. Where have you been?"

"You wouldn't believe it," Clark said. "They had me locked up in this place, and—"

"Where are you now, Roger?" she said.

"I'm at a drive-in on the Strip. Super-burger, it's called."

Another pause. "What do you want me to do?"

"I want to talk to you. I thought if I came over to your place, we could—"

"No, no. It's better if we meet somewhere else. I'll come down. Super-burger?"

"Yes."

"Give me fifteen minutes," she said. When he hung up, he felt an immense sense of relief.

21
IT'S YOU, ROGER

He had a hamburger and settled down to wait, but as he waited, he began to have odd feelings. He didn't like to be suspicious, but . . .

Feeling almost guilty, he drove his car out of the drive-in lot and across the street, parking it a block away, on the hill leading down to the center of town. Then he walked back and stood on the corner across the street from the drive-in.

The night was cool but not cold, and the laughter of the kids was gay and reassuring. When Janice drove up in her Italian sportscar, he felt himself relaxing once more. She was alone; everything was fine. She got out of the car and stood uncertainly, looking around her.

He started to cross the street.

At that moment, he heard the sirens. He froze, moved back to the curb.

Three police cars converged on the Super-burger Drive-in. They pulled up, lights flashing, sirens going. Six cops jumped out, guns drawn.

The kids screamed. The scene was chaotic. There were cries of "Bust! Bust!"

And in the middle of it all, Janice stood frowning and worried-looking. One of the cops came up to her to talk. She answered his questions, shaking her head.

Bitch, he thought, and moved back down the hill. He got into the car and drove off. The night air was making him more clear-headed, and he was remembering more of what had happened to him. He remembered the chair, and the room, and the sounds and fog and shocks. He remembered it dimly, as if it had been a dream.

But it made sense—even as a dream.

Janice, on the other hand. She made no sense at all. Why had she called the cops? And they were cops, no question of it. They weren't fakes. They were real, live, honest-to-God cops.

And they had come very quickly.

Ergo . . .

He was a wanted man. Wanted for what?

He drove half a mile to a gas station, got out, and made another call, this time to Dr. Andrews. A woman answered. He asked for Dr. Andrews. "Dr. Andrews speaking."

"Dr. Andrews, this is Roger Clark."

"Roger?"

"Yes, sir."

"Roger, where are you?"

Dr. Andrews' voice was sympathetic and concerned. But wrong: he never called anyone by his first name. Except patients. Clark shuddered.

"Roger, are you there? Where are you?"

"I'm . . . downtown."

"But where?"

"In a gas station."

"Now look, Roger. I want you to stay where you are. Stay

right where you are, and don't get excited. Everything will be fine. Tell me the address of the gas station."

"Why?" Clark said.

"Now, Roger," Andrews said, chuckling. "This is no time to be difficult. We only want to help you. Tell me where you—"

Clark hung up.

———

So Andrews was part of it, too. What had happened? It must have been awful, whatever it was, if the whole town was after him this way.

Certainly he couldn't go to the police. Not now. Not until he knew more. Then who?

———

He knocked on the door of the pink stucco mansion. A maid answered hesitantly, opening the door just a fraction. "Yes?"

"I want to see Dr. Shine."

"The doctor is not available."

"He is for me. Tell him it's Roger Clark. And tell him to hurry—if he's not out here in a minute, I'll leave. You understand?"

"Yes."

The door was slammed hurriedly in his face. Clark stepped back, onto the grass, until he could look up to the second floor. He saw a light go on, probably the bedroom.

He waited on the grass, standing in the darkness beneath a large tree. After a moment, the door opened, and yellow light spilled out on the lawn. A figure emerged.

"Anybody here?"

He recognized Shine's voice.

"It's me. Roger Clark."

"Oh?" The voice was disbelieving. He moved forward onto the lawn as Shine advanced. Clark could not see anything but the silhouette, framed in yellow light.

"Yes. It's me, all right."

"Where are you? Let me get a look at you."

Clark stepped out from beneath the tree. "I want to talk to you—"

"My God. It *is* Roger Clark."

And Shine fired. There was a spurt of flame from his waist; Clark threw himself to the ground and rolled. Another shot and still another. He rolled across the wet grass, down toward his car.

"Give up, Clark. It's over. You've had it."

Another shot rang out. But by now he had moved away from Shine. He got up and ran for his car, jumping behind the wheel. A shot shattered the rear window. He started the car, and drove off.

In the rear window he saw Shine standing in the street, and then starting to run inside.

Where, he thought, do I go now?

He knocked on the door for five minutes before there was an answer. The door opened; he saw the sleepy face of Jerry Barnes.

"Christ! Roger!"

Clark pushed him aside and entered the apartment. He closed the door behind him and locked it.

Jerry stepped back.

"Now wait a minute, Roger. Just take it easy."

"I'm taking it easy."

"Just relax. I know you've been through a lot, and—"

Jerry was moving toward the phone.

"Don't, Jerry. Don't touch it."

Immediately, he moved back, holding up his hands. "Okay, okay, Rog, take it easy, right?"

Clark sat down. He was suddenly very tired. "Jerry," he said, "what happened?"

"Nothing happened, Rog. Everything's fine. Everything is just—"

"Everything is not fine. The whole damned town is after me. The cops are chasing me. I just got shot at. A nice girl turned me in. Everything is not fine at all."

"Rog, they're worried, that's all. They're concerned about you."

Clark said, "You got any more martinis?"

"Sure. Always. But—"

"Make two," Clark said. "Big ones."

Jerry hesitated, then went into the kitchen. It was clear he was humoring Clark, and that he was afraid of him for some reason.

"Jerry," he said, "do you know the whole story behind all this?"

"Yeah, sure, Rog," Jerry said. "Everybody knows."

"Everybody?"

"Yeah, we thought it was very, uh, disturbing."

"You bet it's disturbing," Clark said. He got up and went into the kitchen, where he heard Jerry pouring the drinks.

"It's disturbing as—"

Abruptly, he was struck on the back of the head.

He fell, in a moment of pain and dizziness, but sat up immediately. Jerry was standing over him with a soda bottle in his hand.

"What the hell did you do that for?" Clark said.

Jerry looked confused. "I was trying . . ."

"To knock me out? Thanks." He rubbed his head, which throbbed painfully.

"It always works in pictures," Jerry said, putting the bottle down.

"Thanks a lot."

"Well, it's for your own good," Jerry said. "You ought to realize you're a sick man. You need time to recover, to get back on an even keel."

"And you were just trying to help," Clark said.

"I don't know," Jerry said. He looked embarrassed. "Here. Take this. Drink it and get the hell out of here." He gave Clark the martini. "It's all I can do for you, Rog."

Clark looked at the martini and continued to rub his head. He was getting nowhere with Jerry. He was getting nowhere with anybody. It was all—

"I'm a sick man?"

"Look, Rog, it's an *illness*. Just like any other kind of illness. You'll get well, but it takes time. We all have faith in you."

"Jerry," he said slowly, "I don't know what you're talking about."

"It was quite a shock to all of us," Jerry said.

"What was?"

"The whole business."

"What business?"

Jerry turned, picked up a newspaper clipping from on top of the refrigerator, and handed it to Clark.

He read it quickly. The headline said DOCTOR COMMITTED. The story was brief and vague, describing how Dr. Roger Clark, a resident at the Los Angeles Memorial Hospital, had attacked a medical secretary, Miss Janice Connor. She had called the police and Clark had been retained in custody by the police; later, when she declined to press charges, he was released into the care of Dr. Harvey Blood for institutional treatment.

"Oh," Clark said.

"I got to admit," Jerry said, "you don't seem too crazy to me, just a little confused."

"You've been clearer yourself," Clark said. He tapped the article with his finger. "This is a frame, Jerry."

"A frame?"

"Yeah. This guy Blood arranged for me to be shipped off to a Caribbean island, where they give the guests all these drugs, and then—"

"Now, Rog . . ."

"It's the truth, I swear it."

"I'm willing to believe you, Rog, but I'm not the one you have to convince."

At that moment, he heard sirens in the distance, but coming closer.

"What's that?"

"What's what?" Jerry said innocently.

"Oh, for Christ's sake," Clark said. He went to the bedroom and looked in. Linda was there, cowering in the bed, still holding the telephone.

"Thanks for everything," Clark said.

He ran.

He drove off just as the first of the police cars pulled up in front of Jerry's apartment building. It was now four in the morning; the first dawn was lightening the sky over the mountains to the east.

Time was very important now. In daylight, they would

have him, and daylight was only a few hours away. He felt his old anger returning, the blind rage which made him sweat and shiver.

He was all alone—he knew that now. Nobody could help him. He had to find a solution by himself, and he had to find it quickly.

To begin with, he needed materials. But where would he find them?

Only one place came to mind: the hospital.

He slipped in through the service entrance, and made his way along the underground tunnels to the elevators. No one saw him; he was alone with his echoing footsteps and the hissing pipes overhead.

At the elevator, he pressed the fourth-floor button, and held it. The doors closed, and the elevator ascended smoothly, without stopping at any intermediate floors.

At the fourth floor, the doors opened. He went out. Directly ahead was a sign: TO OPERATING ROOMS.

This was where he wanted to be.

22
BACK IN THE U.S.S.R.

Down the hallway was the utility closet. He ducked in and found a pair of coveralls and the blue shirt that maintenance men wore; there was also a transistor radio hanging on a peg. The night men often carried a transistor around with them for company. He put on the coveralls and shirt, hung the transistor from the strap around his shoulder, and turned it on.

It was a Beatles song; he paid little attention as he pushed the large utility cart forward. On the cart were several trays of supplies, and a large cloth sack at one end, open at the top, for garbage disposal.

He pushed the cart into the operating area, through the swinging doors, his transistor going full blast. There was a night nurse at the registration desk, next to the large blackboard where the day's operations were scheduled and crossed off when completed; there were two recovery room nurses walking around, and a maintenance man waxing the floors in OR 2.

Nobody paid any attention to him, though the night nurse glanced up when she heard the music. He pushed his cart through to the supply room, and busied himself cleaning out the wastebaskets. A technician was there, hunting among the shelves of supplies that ran from floor to ceiling.

She turned to him. "We're out of Kellys," she said.

"What?"

"We're out of Kellys. Order more from central supply, will you?"

"All right," he said.

The technician left; he was alone in the room. Swiftly, he pushed the cart down to the anesthesia supplies. There were several cans of ether on the lowest shelf. Alongside was a sign: "Authorized Personnel Only."

He scooped up six of the cans and set them onto the shelf of the cart. Then, looking further, he saw a timer used to record the anesthetic induction times; it was a mechanical, spring-wound affair, but quite accurate.

Lastly, he found an oxygen cylinder. It was a small one, just a few cubic feet, but quite heavy. He could carry it under one arm, but it weighed twenty pounds.

He looked around, found the stickers, and pasted one across the cylinder: EMPTY RETURN TO GAS LABORATORY FOR REFILLING.

A few minutes later, he was back in the utility closet, shucking off his coveralls.

"Gee, I had a dreadful flight," went the song on the radio.

He flicked it off, gathered up the equipment, wrapped the coveralls around it, and walked out to the elevator.

Once outside the hospital, he had a moment of elation. He had done it; he had pulled it off. He drove away into the early morning, and as he drove his elation disappeared.

The most difficult part was still ahead.

It took him twenty minutes, driving on back roads and through residential districts, to reach the Santa Monica Freeway. From there, it was twelve minutes to the Los Calos exit. The sun was beginning to appear above the mountains as he turned off the freeway, and onto the small road that led north, to Advance, Inc.

It was quite light when he reached the black sign by the road; he drove a quarter-mile beyond, then pulled the car off the road and into the woods. He walked back to the road and tried to hide the tire tracks, but it was difficult, and he abandoned the attempt after a few minutes.

He returned to the car, got out his material, and crept through the woods toward Advance. It was fifteen minutes before he came to the rise in the hill, and was able to look down over the glass building and the parking lot. There were two police cars in the lot, next to the limousine. The cops were standing around, talking to a short man whom he recognized as Harvey Blood.

They seemed to be having an argument; Blood was waving his hands and speaking earnestly, while the cops stood around frowning.

He looked from the parking lot toward the building itself, his eyes going along the ground floor windows to those of his own lab. He usually left one window open, though he was not supposed to. He hated stuffy labs in the morning.

He saw the window: he was in luck. It was open.

Back at the parking lot, Blood seemed to be winning his argument. The cops shrugged and climbed into their cars, and drove off. One, however, remained behind, standing at the entrance to the building.

As the police cars left, Harvey Blood went into the building. The cop remained outside. He took his gun from his holster, checked it, and put it back, leaving the flap loose.

In the early morning light, he practiced a quick draw, then nodded to himself, apparently satisfied, and sat down on the steps.

Clark waited.

A light went on in Harvey Blood's office.

Clark moved down the hillside.

He had planned to move stealthily; he envisioned himself sliding like a silent shadow down the hill. Instead, he stumbled and fell, rolling over and over, the heavy oxygen cylinder clanging on the rocks.

At the foot of the hill, winded, ribs aching, he paused. The sound had seemed unbearably loud: the cop at the front of the building must have heard.

He scrambled forward to his open window, pushed it wide, and looked into the lab. The lights were out and the lab was empty. He pushed his equipment through the window, easing it gently to the floor. Then he climbed up and through, dropping down and waiting.

Two minutes passed, and then the cop appeared. He was walking along the rear of the building, gun out, eyes up to the hillside.

Clark could see the track he had left coming down the hill. The long grass was trampled in an unmistakable path. He held his breath and waited.

The cop didn't notice. He moved on.

Clark continued to wait, huddled down on the floor, his face pressed up against the cool oxygen bottle. Another three minutes passed, and the cop returned, walking back around to the front.

When he was finally gone, Clark stood. He walked around

the benches of the lab, searching for something that would do the trick. He needed something that would work slowly . . .

The hot plate.

He paused. Perfect!

It was a simple hot plate, a single burner of the kind used by little old ladies in retirement apartments. In the lab, it was employed to heat reagents and bottles of liquid. It had a single coil which glowed red-hot in a matter of minutes.

Perfect.

He spent the next few moments cutting the wires to the coil, and hooking them into the anesthesia timer. He wasn't sure about the connections, but there was no time to make them more secure. Glancing at his watch, he saw that it was already six-fifteen.

No time.

He collected all his gear and looked around him. He needed an airtight room now, a perfectly airtight room. His own lab would never do.

But he knew someplace that would.

Fortunately, he had kept the keychain from Sam, the night guard, so he had keys to open any room in the building. It was the work of a few moments to slip down the hallway and into George K. Washington's lab.

He hesitated as he entered. Directly ahead were the chair, the tracks, and the door leading to the soundproofed room. He felt a kind of deep revulsion, and for an instant he thought he could not make himself enter the room. Then he heard footsteps outside, and Harvey Blood's voice saying, ". . . be back, I know he will . . ."

Clark smiled grimly.

He opened the door to the soundproofed room, and set the hot plate on the ground, resting it on the baffles. He plugged it into a socket, and twisted the timer to fifteen minutes. It began ticking softly.

Then, he set the oxygen cylinder on the floor nearby, and opened the valve a half turn. He heard a hissing and felt the coolness of the gas.

Finally, he took the small cylinders of ether, pulled the corks, and sprinkled the liquid around the room. The burning, acrid odor of ether stung his nostrils and made his eyes water; after two cans, he was not sure he could go on, it was making him dizzy, but he forced himself.

He managed to empty six cylinders, and threw in a seventh for good measure.

Then, coughing, he went back, and slammed the door shut. It closed heavily.

He checked his watch: fourteen minutes left.

It was not, he thought, the best explosive in the world, but it would do. Ether and air was reasonably powerful; ether and oxygen, pure oxygen, would be extremely potent. The enclosed space of the room would do the rest.

When that room exploded, it would really go. Smiling, he went back to his lab.

As he took the pink vial off the shelf and mixed two grams in water, a part of him was horrified. The deliberate cruelty of it shocked him. But another part of him was pleased and excited by what he was about to do.

In a way, he thought, it was fitting. He mixed the solution, and filled a syringe. Then he slipped on a labcoat, dropped the syringe in his pocket, and went to pay a final visit on Harvey Blood.

There were eleven minutes left.

"Hello, Roger," Harvey Blood said calmly, looking up from his desk. "I see you're back."

"Yes," Clark said. "I'm back."

"You led the police a merry chase, Roger."

"Yes. I did."

"But I knew you'd come back," Blood said. "I knew it all along. You see, Roger, we arranged everything so that you would *have* to come back."

"Yes," Clark said. "That's true."

"The effects of our treatment wore off," Blood said. "We knew it was happening. We watched you change for the last few weeks. We knew that eventually you would do this, and we were prepared for it."

"Prepared?"

"Yes. In fact, we've been counting on you to make your escape, and to act in a bizarre fashion. Which, naturally, you did. We needed that for legal reasons."

"What reasons?"

Blood sighed. "Poor Roger. You never will understand, will you? We needed this final evidence in order to certify you insane."

Harvey Blood sat back in his chair and looked steadily at Clark. "The corporation is overextended," he said. "Now do you understand?"

Clark sat down. "No."

"We had very good initial success, with some viruses which we sold to the government. Then we developed the drug, and put it to use in the resort. Another success. We grew bolder—began branching out, working on a wide variety of projects. We accepted contracts from a number of companies. Contracts, Roger, which we have been unable to fill."

Clark frowned.

"In fact," Blood said, "we began to find ourselves in great financial trouble. So much trouble, that our good projects—the ones that were panning out, the ones that promised success, the ones like Glow Girl—couldn't be properly funded. Glow Girl was initially planned for a million. Yesterday, we found that we had only eighty thousand available for it. It's embarrassing, Roger. Very embarrassing. Half our projects aren't working out, and the others we can't finance."

Clark glanced at his watch.

"How much time?" Harvey Blood asked mildly.

Clark said nothing.

"Oh, there's no point in trying to hide it. We know what's happening. For example," he said, "I just got a call from the police. They notified me that the LA Memorial Hospital had just been robbed. A peculiar robbery—some ether and some oxygen. Now who would take ether and oxygen, Roger?"

Clark felt everything sliding away from him, his plans, his preparations, all of it disappearing into some awful master plan.

"I've been a fool," he said.

There were ten minutes left.

23
FOOLS WALK OUT

"Not a fool, Roger," Harvey Blood said. "Just nearsighted. You mustn't let it depress you. It could have happened to anybody. Speaking for the corporation, I must say we are all very pleased at the way you've worked out. You've been a great help to us, a great help. And now, when you destroy this building, you will have performed an invaluable service. We can't thank you enough."

There was still time, Clark thought, to go back and pull the plug. Still time to call it off . . .

"The fact is," Blood continued, "that we've removed all our notes and data from the building. We did it four days ago, because we knew you'd make your move soon. Assuming you are an efficient deviser of homemade bombs—and ether and oxygen should be efficient enough—we can expect this entire building to be demolished. Think what that will mean: no building, no labs, nothing. Obviously we cannot complete our contractual obligations. Obviously, the insurance clauses which cover such contracts will be invoked. And obviously, the insurance on this building itself—five million dollars, and a little more—will go far toward financing our viable projects. So you see, it will all work out nicely."

Clark found his voice at last. "And me?"

"Well, I admit you pose a problem. You're quite mad. You've attacked a girl, you escaped from my care and flew around the Caribbean, and now you escaped again, threatening friends and acquaintances. And to climax it all, you destroy a corporation. Quite mad. I have no doubt that the courts will find you homicidal and destructive in the extreme, and will want to institutionalize you in a state hospital."

"I see. But I'll—"

"Talk? You will indeed. And that is why you pose a problem."

"You're going to kill me."

"Well, not immediately, Roger. Not immediately."

Clark stood up. "You have it all worked out," he said. "You've always had it worked out, from the very beginning."

"We like to think so," Blood said.

Silently, Clark removed the syringe from his pocket and set it on the desk. The pink liquid was clearly visible.

"Have you thought about this?" he asked.

Harvey Blood did not move. His face was expressionless as he stared at the syringe.

"Roger, you're being foolish."

"I think I'm finally being smart."

"Roger, there's no need—"

"I disagree." Clark picked up the syringe and held it to the light, squeezing the plunger slightly so that the air bubbles were pushed out. A fine stream of liquid shot into the air.

"Roger, that's a large dose—"

Blood was reaching into the desk drawer. In a swift movement, Clark came around the desk, shoved the drawer shut with his knee. Blood screamed.

Clark jabbed the needle into Blood's arm, right through his clothing. He felt it enter the skin and muscle; he squeezed out the contents.

Blood did not move. His mouth fell open in horror, and he clutched his arm.

Clark pushed him away from the desk, opened the drawer, and removed the gun. Alongside it in the drawer was a small tuning fork.

He held it up to Blood and smiled.

"Listen, Roger," Harvey Blood said, speaking very rapidly, "listen, we can work something out."

"No, we can't."

"Listen, Roger, you're being ridiculous. If you think by all this that you can stop the corporation—"

"I can stop you."

"—you're wrong. I'm not alone. Advance is not alone. All over the country, corporations are springing up. What we don't do, somebody else will carry out. It's impossible to stop us. It's the wave of the future. It's coming, like it or not."

Clark held the tuning fork loosely in his hand.

"Don't you see?" Harvey Blood said. "Don't you understand? You're fighting for a principle that doesn't exist. Already you are manipulated, pushed, pulled, tugged by your world. Do you think a car is beautiful? If you do, it is only because somebody paid millions in advertising to make you think so. Do you find a woman attractive? If you do, it is only because someone planned the fashion, the clothing, the walk, the talk—"

"No," Clark said. "You're wrong."

"Are you against drugs? If you are, you're in the minority.

The largest-selling prescription drugs in this country are tranquilizers and sedatives. *Everybody* takes them. Everybody wants them. Everybody loves—"

"No," Clark said. "You're wrong."

"Do you want to live in a certain neighborhood? Do you find certain food tasty? Do you prefer certain climates, clothes, cars, paintings, movies, books, films, toilet paper, soap, toothpaste, singers? Don't you see your preferences are all conditioned? Don't you see you are manipulated every minute of your life? You're manipulated by Procter and Gamble, by Ford, by MGM, by Random House, by Brooks, by Bergdorf, by Revlon, by Upjohn—"

"No," Clark said. "You're wrong."

"I'm right," Harvey Blood said, sweat pouring down his face. His eyes were fixed on the tuning fork. "I swear to God I'm right."

"You're wrong," Clark said, and struck the tuning fork against the desk.

It hummed softly.

Harvey Blood did not move. He continued to stare at Clark, and his lips worked, but he did not speak. Clark watched with a kind of curiosity: he had never given the reversal drug in such a large dose before.

Harvey Blood screamed.

"They're after me!" he cried. "They're all after me!"

He sobbed, tears running down his cheeks. And then he began to pound his head against the desk.

Clark looked at his watch.

Four minutes.

He walked out of the room, hearing Harvey Blood's cries, and the sound of his head thumping against polished mahogany.

The rest went quite smoothly. He hit the policeman at the front door across the back of the skull, then carried him, feet scraping, across the asphalt parking lot, dropping him onto the wet grass some distance from the building.

Three minutes.

He climbed into the limousine and started the engine. As he was about to pull out of the parking lot, a small sportscar came up and stopped by the entrance. A girl got out; he recognized Susan Ryle.

He called to her. She came over, frowning. "What's going on?"

"There's about to be an explosion," he said, pointing to the building. "Right in there."

"An explosion? What are you talking about?"

"Get into the car," he said.

She hesitated.

"Get in!"

She climbed into the back seat. He checked his watch: a little more than two minutes.

He drove down to the road, turned left, and went two hundred yards. He pulled off and waited. From here, they could still see the building.

She said, "You're really serious." Her voice was awed and frightened.

"I really am, Susan."

"My name isn't Susan now. It's Angela Sweet."

"Sorry," he said. "It's Susan once again."

The seconds ticked by. Finally Susan said, "How do you know there's going to be—"

She stopped. She understood. "You're a madman," she said.

"Apparently." He grinned.

"*You're* going to blow up that building?"

"Apparently."

One minute left. He sighed.

"But you can't do that. Everything is there—my costumes, the music, everything."

He shrugged. "The breaks."

"How can you do this to me?" she wailed, and began to cry.

At that moment, the headquarters of Advance, Inc. exploded. Clark thought it was rather a nice explosion, one that built up slowly from a muffled roar to a giant hot fireball as chemical stores caught and blew. The building seemed to fly apart; the sky was filled with gas and burning sparks.

Susan watched, mouth open, and then sobbed loudly. "I hate you," she said. "I hate you, I hate you, I hate you."

"That's all right."

"I hope when they catch you they lock you up and throw away the key."

"They may do that," he said, starting the car and driving down the road.

"You're completely insane," she said. "Hopelessly insane."

"That will be decided," he said. He turned onto the freeway, and headed toward the police station. As he drove, he wondered if she were right. He wondered if he were really insane.

He decided that probably, he wasn't.

But it was hard to be sure.

Christiansted, St. Croix
January 1969